"You don't want to marry me. You don't want to marry anybody!"

"But the bottom line is that unless we marry, I won't be around *enough*," Angel intoned with grim emphasis. "I want my daughter to learn what it means to be a Valtinos..."

"Well, that's going to be rather awkward when it's not what I want and I will fight you every step of the way!" Merry flung back at him. "You wanted me out of your life and I got out. You can't force me back."

"If it means my daughter gets the future she deserves, I will force you," Angel growled, yanking her up against him, shifting his lithe hips, ensuring she recognized how turned-on he was. "You make me want you."

"It's *my* fault?" Merry caroled in disbelief even as her whole body tilted into his. She wanted to slap herself, she wanted to slap him, she wanted to freeze the moment and replay it *her* way, in which she would say something terribly clever and wounding that would hold him at bay.

And then he kissed her, crushing her ripe mouth, his tongue plunging and retreating, and she saw stars and whirling multicoloured planets behind her lowered lids while her body fizzed like a fireworks display, leaving her weak with hunger. She kissed him back, hands rising to delve into the crisp luxuriance of his hair, framing, holding, *needing*. It was frantic, out of control, the way it always was for them.

Vows for Billionaires

His heir, in exchange for his ring!

Angel Valtinos, Prince Vitale Castiglione and Zac Da Rocha have more than just a father in common—these three billionaires have reputations for ruthless command! No women have ever breached their defenses. But they're about to be faced with unexpected consequences...

To legitimize their legacies, they must strike a deal. But will a vow be enough for the mothers of their children—or will they need passion to walk down the aisle?

The Secret Valtinos Baby

Available now!

Vitale and Jasmine's story

Available April 2018

Zac and Freddie's story

Available June 2018

Lynne Graham

THE SECRET VALTINOS BABY

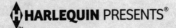

HARLEQUIN PRESENTS®

Recycling programs
for this product may
not exist in your area.

ISBN-13: 978-1-335-41908-8

The Secret Valtinos Baby

First North American Publication 2018

Copyright © 2018 by Lynne Graham

Printed in U.S.A.

Lynne Graham was born in Northern Ireland and has been a keen romance reader since her teens. She is very happily married to an understanding husband who has learned to cook since she started to write! Her five children keep her on her toes. She has a very large dog who knocks everything over, a very small terrier who barks a lot and two cats. When time allows, Lynne is a keen gardener.

Books by Lynne Graham

Harlequin Presents

Bought for the Greek's Revenge
The Sicilian's Stolen Son
Leonetti's Housekeeper Bride

Wedlocked!

His Queen by Desert Decree
Claimed for the Leonelli Legacy

Brides for the Taking

The Desert King's Blackmailed Bride
The Italian's One-Night Baby
Sold for the Greek's Heir

Christmas with a Tycoon

The Italian's Christmas Child
The Greek's Christmas Bride

The Notorious Greeks

The Greek Demands His Heir
The Greek Commands His Mistress

Bound by Gold

The Billionaire's Bridal Bargain
The Sheikh's Secret Babies

Visit the Author Profile page at Harlequin.com for more titles.

CHAPTER ONE

THE GREEK BILLIONAIRE, Angel Valtinos, strode into his father's office suite to find both his brothers waiting in Reception and he stopped dead, ebony brows skating up. 'What is this? A family reunion?'

'Or Papa is planning to carpet us for something,' his Italian half-brother, Prince Vitale Castiglione, commented with perceptible amusement because they were all beyond the age where parental disapproval was a normal source of concern.

'Does he make a habit of that?' Zac Da Rocha demanded with a frown.

Angel met Vitale's eyes and his jawline squared, neither passing comment. Zac, their illegitimate Brazilian sibling, was pretty much a wild card. As he was a new and rather mysterious addition to the family circle his brothers had yet to fully accept him. And trust came no more easily to the suspicious Angel than it did to Vitale.

Vitale grinned. 'You're the eldest,' he reminded Angel. 'You get top billing and first appearance.'

'Not sure I want it on this occasion,' Angel conceded, but he swiftly shrugged off the faint and comically unfamiliar sense of unease assailing his innately rock-solid confidence.

After all, Charles Russell had *never* played the heavy father in his sons' lives, but even without exercising that authority he had still been a remarkably decent father, Angel conceded reflectively. Charles had not stayed married to either his or Vitale's mother for very long but he had taken a keen interest post-divorce in fostering and maintaining a close relationship with his sons. Angel had often had cause to be grateful for his father's stable approach to life and the shrewd business brain he suspected he had inherited from him. His mother was a thoroughly flighty and frivolous Greek heiress, whose attitude to childcare and education would have been careless without his father's stipulations on his son's behalf.

Charles Russell crossed his office to greet his eldest son. 'You're late,' he told him without heat.

'My board meeting ran over,' Angel told him smoothly. 'What's this all about? When I saw Zac and Vitale in Reception I wondered if there was a family emergency.'

'It depends what you call an emergency,' Charles deflected, studying his very tall thirty-three-year-old eldest son, who topped him in height by several inches.

A son to be proud of, Charles had believed until very recently when the startling discovery of certain disquieting information had punctured his paternal pride. To be fair, Angel also carried the genes of a fabulously wealthy and pedigreed Greek family, more known for their self-destructiveness than their achievements. Even so, Charles had prided himself on Angel's hugely successful reputation in the business world. Angel was the first Valtinos in two generations to make more money than he spent. A very astute high-achiever and a loyal and loving son, he was the very last child Charles had expected to disappoint him. Nonetheless, Angel had let him down by revealing a ruthless streak of Valtinos self-interest and irresponsibility.

'Tell me what this is about,' Angel urged with characteristic cool.

Charles rested back against his tidy desk, a still handsome man with greying hair in his early fifties. His well-built frame was tense. 'When do you plan to grow up?' he murmured wryly.

Angel blinked in bewilderment. 'Is that a joke?' he whispered.

'Sadly not,' his father confirmed. 'A week ago, I learned from a source I will not share that I am a *grandfather...*'

Angel froze, his lean, extravagantly handsome features suddenly wiped clean of all animation, while his shrewd dark eyes hardened and veiled. In less than a split second, though, he had lifted his aggressive chin in grim acknowledgement of the unwelcome shock he had been dealt: an issue he had hoped to keep buried had been unexpectedly and most unhappily disinterred by the only man in the world whose good opinion he valued.

'And, moreover, the grandfather of a child whom I will never meet if you have anything to do with it,' Charles completed in a tone of regret.

Angel frowned and suddenly extended his arms in a very expansive Greek gesture of dismissal. 'I thought to protect you—'

'No, your sole motivation was to protect *you*,' Charles contradicted without hesitation. 'From the demands and responsibility of a child.'

'It was an accident. Am I expected to turn my life upside down when struck by such a misfortune?' Angel demanded in a tone of raw self-defence.

His father dealt him a troubled appraisal. 'I did not consider *you* to be a misfortune.'

'Your relationship with my mother was on rather a different footing,' Angel declared with all the pride of his wealthy, privileged forebears.

A deep frown darkened the older man's face. 'Angel... I've never told you the whole truth about my marriage to your mother because I did not want to give you cause to respect her less,' he admitted reluctantly. 'But the fact is that Angelina deliberately conceived you once she realised that I wanted to end our relationship. I married her because she was pregnant, *not* because I loved her.'

Angel was startled by that revelation but not shocked, for he had always been aware that his mother was spoilt and selfish and that she could not handle rejection. His luxuriant black lashes lifted on challenging and cynical dark golden eyes. 'And marrying her didn't work for you, did it? So, you can hardly be suggesting that I marry the mother of *my* child!' he derided.

'No, marrying Angelina Valtinos didn't work for me,' Charles agreed mildly. 'But it worked beautifully for *you*. It gave you a father with the right to interfere and with your best interests always at heart.'

That retaliation was a stunner and shockingly true and Angel gritted his even white teeth at the comeback. 'Then I should thank you for your sacrifice,' he said hoarsely.

'No thanks required. The wonderful little boy grew up into a man I respect—'

'With the obvious exception of this issue,' Angel interjected tersely.

'You have handled it all wrong. You called in the lawyers, those Valtinos vulture lawyers, whose sole motivation is to protect you and the Valtinos name and fortune—'

'Exactly,' Angel slotted in softly. 'They protect me.'

'But don't you *want* to know your own child?' Charles demanded in growing frustration.

Angel compressed his wide, sensual mouth, his hard bone structure thrown into prominence, angry shame engulfing him at that question. 'Of course, I do, but getting past her mother is proving difficult.'

'Is that how you see it? Is that who you are blaming for this mess?' the older man countered with scorn. 'Your lawyers forced her to sign a non-disclosure agreement in return for financial support and you made no attempt at that point to show enough interest to arrange access to your child.'

Angel went rigid, battling his anger, determined not to surrender to the frustrating rage scorching through him. He was damned if he was about to let the maddening baby business, as he thought of it, come between him and the father he loved. 'The child hadn't been born at that stage. I had no idea how I would feel once she was.'

'Your lawyers naturally concentrated on protecting your privacy and your wealth. Your role was to concentrate on the *family* aspect,' Charles asserted with emphasis. 'Instead you have made an enemy of your child's mother.'

'That was not my intention. Using the Valtinos legal team was intended to remove any damaging personal reactions from our dealings.'

'And how has the impersonal approach worked for you?' Charles enquired very drily indeed.

Angel very nearly groaned out loud in exasperation. In truth, he had played an own goal, getting what he'd believed he wanted and then discovering too late that it wasn't what he wanted at all. 'She doesn't want me to visit.'

'And whose fault is that?'

'Mine,' Angel acknowledged fiercely. 'But she is currently raising my child in unsuitable conditions.'

'Yes, working as a kennel maid while raising the next Valtinos heiress isn't to be recommended,' his father remarked wryly. 'Well, at least the woman's not a gold-digger. A gold-digger would have stayed in London and lived the high life on the income you provided, not stranded herself in rural Suffolk with a middle-aged aunt while working for a living.'

'My daughter's mother is *crazy*!' Angel bit out, betraying his first real emotion on the subject. 'She's trying to make me feel bad!'

Charles raised a dubious brow. 'You think so? Seems to be a lot of sweat and effort to go to for a man she refuses to see.'

'She had the neck to tell my lawyer that she couldn't allow me to visit without risking breaching the non-disclosure agreement!' Angel growled.

'There could be grounds for that concern,' his father remarked thoughtfully. 'The paparazzi do follow you around and you visiting her *would* put a spotlight on her and the child.'

Angel drew himself up to his full six feet four inches and squared his wide shoulders. 'I would be discreet.'

'Sadly, it's a little late in the day to be fighting over parental access. You should have considered that first and foremost in your dealings because unmarried fathers have few, if any, rights under British law—'

'Are you suggesting that I marry her?' Angel demanded with incredulity.

'No.' Charles shook his greying head to emphasise that negative. 'That sort of gesture has to come from the heart.'

'Or the brain,' Angel qualified. 'I could marry her, take her out to Greece and then fight her there for custody, where I would have an advantage. That option *was* suggested at one point by my legal team.'

Charles regarded his unapologetically ruthless son with concealed apprehension because it had never been his intention to exacerbate the situation between his son and the mother of his child. 'I would hope that you would not even consider sinking to that level of deceit. Surely a more enlightened arrangement is still possible?'

But *was* it? Angel was not convinced even while he assured his concerned father that he would sort the situation out without descending to the level of dirty tricks. But was an access agreement even achievable?

After all, how could he be sure of anything in that line? Merry Armstrong had foiled him, blocked him and denied him while subjecting him to a raft of outrageous arguments rather than simply giving him what he wanted. Angel was wholly unaccustomed to such disrespectful treatment. Every time she knocked him back he was stunned by the unfamiliarity of the experience.

All his life he had pretty much got what he wanted from a woman whenever he wanted it. Women, usually, adored him. Women from his mother to his aunts to his cousins and those in his bed worshipped him like a god. Women lived to please Angel, flatter him, satisfy him: it had always been that way in Angel's gilded world of comfort and pleasure. And Angel had taken that enjoyable reality entirely for granted until the very dark day he had chosen to tangle with Merry Armstrong…

He had noticed her immediately, the long glossy mane of dark mahogany hair clipped in a ponytail that reached almost to her waist, the pale crystalline blue eyes and the pink voluptuous mouth that sang of sin to a sexually imaginative male. Throw in the lean, leggy lines of a greyhound and proximity and their collision course had been inevitable from day one in spite of the fact that he had never before slept with one of his employees and had always sworn *not* to do so.

Merry's fingers closed shakily over the letter that the postman had just delivered. A tatty sausage-shaped Yorkshire terrier gambolled noisily round her feet, still overexcited by the sound of the doorbell and another voice.

'Quiet, Tiger,' Merry murmured firmly, mindful that fostering the little dog was aimed at making him a suitable adoptee for a new owner. But even as she thought that, she knew she had broken her aunt Sybil's strict rules with Tiger by getting attached and by letting him sneak onto her sofa and up onto her lap. Sybil adored dogs but she didn't believe in humanising or coddling them. It crossed Merry's mind that perhaps she was as emotionally damaged as Tiger had been by abuse. Tiger craved food as comfort; Merry craved the cosiness of a doggy cuddle. Or was she kidding herself in equating the humiliation she had suffered at Angel's hands with abuse? Making a mountain out of a molehill, as Sybil had once briskly told her?

Sadly the proof of that pudding was in the eating as she flipped over the envelope and read the London postmark with a stomach that dive-bombed in sick dismay. It was another legal letter and she couldn't face it. With a shudder of revulsion laced with fear she cravenly thrust the envelope in the drawer of the battered hall table, where it could stay until she felt able to deal with it…*calmly*.

And a calm state of mind had become a challenge for Merry ever since she had first heard from the Valtinoses' lawyers and dealt with the stress, the appointments and the complaints. Legally she seemed mired in a never-ending battle where everything she did was an excuse for criticism or another unwelcome and intimidating demand. She could feel the rage building in her at the prospect of having to open yet another politely menacing letter, a rage that she would not have recognised a mere year earlier, a rage that threatened to consume her and sometimes scared her because there had been nothing of the virago in her nature until her path crossed that of Angel Valtinos. He had taught her nothing but bitterness, hatred and resentment, all of which she could have done without.

But he had also, although admittedly *very* reluctantly, given her Elyssa…

Keen to send her thoughts in a less sour direction, Merry glanced from the kitchen into the tiny sitting room of the cottage where she lived, and studied her daughter where she sat on the hearth rug happily engaged with her toys. Her black hair was an explosion of curls round her cherubic olive-toned face, highlighting striking ice-blue eyes and a pouty little mouth. She had her father's curls and her mother's eyes and mouth and was an extremely pretty baby in Merry's opinion, although she was prepared to admit that she was very biased when it came to her daughter.

In many ways after a very fraught and unhappy pregnancy Elyssa's actual birth had restored Merry to startling life and vigour. Before that day, it had not once occurred to her that her daughter's arrival would transform her outlook and fill her to overflowing with an unconditional love unlike anything she had ever felt before. Nowadays she recognised the truth: there was nothing she would not do for Elyssa.

A light knock sounded on the back door, announcing Sybil's casual entrance into the kitchen at the rear of the cottage. 'I'll put on the kettle… time for a brew,' she said cheerfully, a tall, rangy blonde nearing sixty but still defiantly beautiful, as befitted a woman who had been an international supermodel in the eighties.

Sybil had been Merry's role model from an early age. Her mother, Natalie, had married when Merry was sixteen and emigrated to Australia with her husband, leaving her teenaged daughter in her sister's care. Sybil and Merry were much closer than Merry had ever been with her birth mother but Sybil remained very attached to her once feckless kid sister. The sanctuary had been built by her aunt on the proceeds of the modelling career she had abandoned as soon as she had made enough money to devote her days to looking after homeless dogs.

In the later stages of her pregnancy, Merry had worked at the centre doing whatever was required and had lived with her aunt in her trendy barn conversion, but at the same time Merry had been carefully making plans for a more independent future. A qualified accountant, she had started up a small home business doing accounts for local traders and she had a good enough income now to run a car, while also insisting on paying a viable rent to Sybil for her use of the cottage at the gates of the rescue centre. The cottage was small and old-fashioned but it had two bedrooms and a little garden and perfectly matched Merry and Elyssa's current needs.

In fact, Sybil Armstrong was a rock of unchanging affection and security in Merry's life. Merry's mother, Natalie, had fallen pregnant with her during an affair with her married employer. Only nineteen at the time, Natalie had quickly proved ill-suited to the trials of single parenthood. Right from the start, Sybil had regularly swooped in as a weekend babysitter, wafting Merry back to her country home to leave her kid sister free to go out clubbing.

Natalie's bedroom door had revolved around a long succession of unsuitable men. There had been violent men, drunk men, men who took drugs and men who stole Natalie's money and refused to earn their own. By the time she was five years old, Merry had assumed all mothers brought different men home every week. In such an unstable household where fights and substance abuse were endemic she had missed a lot of school, and when social workers had threatened to take Merry into care, once again her aunt had stepped in to take charge.

For nine glorious years, Merry had lived solely with Sybil, catching up with her schoolwork, learning to be a child again, no longer expected to cook and clean for her unreliable mother, no longer required to hide in her bedroom while the adults downstairs screamed so loudly at each other that the neighbours called the police. Almost inevitably that phase of security with Sybil had ended when Natalie had made yet another fresh start and demanded the return of her daughter.

It hadn't worked, of course it hadn't, because Natalie had grown too accustomed to her freedom by then, and instead of finding in Merry the convenient little best friend she had expected she had been met with a daughter with whom she had nothing in common. By the time Keith, who was younger than Natalie, had entered her life, the writing had been on the wall. Keen to return to Australia and take Natalie with him, he had been frank about his reluctance to take on a paternal role while still in his twenties. Merry had moved back in with Sybil and had not seen her mother since her departure.

* * *

'Did I see the postman?' Sybil asked casually.

Merry stiffened and flushed, thinking guiltily of that envelope stuffed in the hall table. 'I bought something for Elyssa online,' she fibbed in shame, but there was just no way she could admit to a woman as gutsy as Sybil that a letter could frighten and distress her.

'No further communication from He Who Must Not Be Named?' Sybil fished, disconcerting her niece with that leading question, for lately her aunt had been very quiet on that topic.

'Evidently we're having a bit of a break from the drama right now, which is really nice,' Merry mumbled, shamefacedly tucking teabags into the mugs while Sybil lifted her great-niece off the rug and cuddled her before sitting down again with the baby cradled on her lap.

'Don't even think about him.'

'I don't,' Merry lied yet again, a current of self-loathing assailing her because only a complete fool would waste time thinking about a man who had mistreated her. But then, really, what would Sybil understand about that? As a staggeringly beautiful and famous young woman, Sybil had had to beat adoring men off with sticks but had simply never met one she wanted to settle down with. Merry

doubted that any man had ever disrespected Sybil
and lived to tell the tale.

'He'll get his comeuppance some day,' Sybil
forecast. 'Everyone does. What goes around comes
around.'

'But it bothers me that I hate him so much,'
Merry confided in a rush half under her breath.
'I've never been a hater before.'

'You're still hurting. Now that you're starting
to date again, those bad memories will soon sink
into the past.'

An unexpected smile lit Merry's heart-shaped
face at the prospect of the afternoon out she was
having the following day. As a veterinary surgeon,
Fergus Wickham made regular visits to the rescue
centre. He had first met Merry when she was off-
puttingly pregnant, only evidently it had not put
him off, it had merely made him bide his time until
her daughter was born and she was more likely to
be receptive to an approach.

She *liked* Fergus, she enjoyed his company, she
reminded herself doggedly. He didn't give her butterflies in her tummy, though, or make her long
for his mouth, she conceded guiltily, but then how
important were such physical feelings in the over-
all scheme of things? Angel's sexual allure had
been the health equivalent of a lethal snakebite,

pulling her in only to poison her. Beautiful but deadly. Dear heaven, she hated him, she acknowledged, rigid with the seething trapped emotion that sent her memory flying inexorably back sixteen months…

CHAPTER TWO

MERRY WAS FULL of enthusiasm when she started her first job even though it wasn't her dream job by any stretch of the imagination. Having left university with a first-class honours degree in accountancy and business, she had no intention of settling permanently into being a front-desk receptionist at Valtinos Enterprises.

Even so, she had badly needed paid employment and the long recruitment process involved in graduate job applications had ensured that she was forced to depend on Sybil's generosity for more months than she cared to count. Sybil had already supported Merry through her years as a student, helping her out with handy vacation jobs at the rescue centre while always providing her with a comfortable home to come back to for weekends and holidays.

Her job at Valtinos Enterprises was Merry's

first step towards true independence. The work paid well and gave her the breathing space in which to look for a more suitable position, while also enabling her to base herself in London without relying on her aunt's financial help. She had moved into a room in a grotty apartment and started work at VE with such high hopes.

And on her first day Angel strode out of the lift and her breath shorted out in her chest as though she had been punched. He had luxuriant black curls that always looked messy and that lean, darkly beautiful face of his had been crafted by a creative genius with exotic high cheekbones, a narrow, straight nose and eyes the colour of liquid honey. Eyes that she had only very much later discovered could turn as hard and cutting as black diamonds.

'You're new,' he commented, treating her to the kind of lingering appraisal that made her feel hot all over.

'This is my first day, Mr Valtinos,' she confided.

'Don't waste your smiles there,' her co-worker on the desk whispered snidely as Angel walked into his office. 'He doesn't flirt with employees. In fact the word is that he's fired a couple of his PAs for getting too personal with him.'

'I'm not interested,' Merry countered with

amusement, and indeed when it came to men she rarely was.

Growing up watching her mother continually search for the man of her dreams while ignoring everything else life had to offer had scared Merry. Having survived her unsettled childhood, she set a high value on security and she was keen to establish her own accountancy firm. She didn't take risks…ever. In fact she was the most risk-averse person she had ever met.

That innate caution had kept her working so hard at university that she had taken little part in the social whirl. There had been occasional boyfriends but none she had cared to invite into her bed. Not only had she never felt passion, but she had also never suffered from her mother's blazing infatuations. Watching relationships around her take off and then fail in an invariably nasty ending that smashed friendships and caused pain and resentment had turned Merry off even more. She liked a calm, tidy life, a *quiet* life, which in no way explained how she could ever have become intimate with a male as volatile as Angel, she acknowledged with lingering bewilderment.

But it was the truth, the absolute truth, that on paper she and Angel were a horrendous match. Angel was off-the-charts volatile with a volcanic hot temper that erupted every time someone did or said something he considered stupid. He wasn't tolerant or easy to deal with. In the first weeks of her employment she regularly saw members of his personal staff race out of his office as though they had wings on their feet, their pale faces stamped with stress and trepidation. He was very impatient and equally demanding. He might resemble a supermodel in his fabulously sophisticated designer suits, but he had the temperament of a tyrant and an overachiever's appetite for work and success. The only thing she admired about him in those initial weeks was his cleverness.

Serving coffee in the boardroom, she heard him dissect entire arguments with a handful of well-chosen words. She noticed that people listened when he spoke and admired his intellect while competing to please and impress him. Occasionally beautiful shapely blondes would drift in to meet him for lunch, women of a definite type, the artificial socialite type, seemingly chosen only for their enviable faces and figures and their ability to look at him with stunned appreciation. Those who arrived without an invite didn't even get across the threshold of his office. He treated women like casual amusements and discarded them as soon as he got bored, and the procession of constantly changing faces made it obvious that he got bored very quickly and easily.

In short, nothing about Angel Valtinos *should* have attracted Merry. He shamelessly flaunted almost every flaw she disliked in a man. He was a selfish, hubristic, oversexed workaholic, spoiled by a life of luxury and the target of more admiration and attention than was good for him.

But even after six weeks in his radius, dredging her eyes off Angel when he was within view had proved impossible. He commanded a room simply by walking into it. Even his voice was dark, deep and smoulderingly charismatic. Once a woman heard that slumberous accented drawl she just had to turn her head and look. His dynamic personality suffused his London headquarters like an energy bolt while his mercurial moods kept his employees on edge and eager to please. Valtinos Enterprises felt dead and flat when he was abroad.

When one of Angel's personal assistants left and the position was offered internally, Merry applied, keen to climb the ladder. Angel summoned her to his office to study her with frowning dark golden eyes. 'Why is a candidate with your skills working on Reception?' he demanded impatiently.

'It was the first job I was offered,' Merry admitted, brushing her damp palms down over her skirt. 'I was planning to move on.'

Rising to his feet, making her uneasily aware of his height, he extended a slim file. 'Find somewhere quiet to work. You're off Reception for the morning. Check out this business and provide me with an accurate assessment of its financial history and current performance. If you do it well, I'll interview you this afternoon.'

That afternoon, he settled the file back on the desk and surveyed her, his wide, sensual mouth compressing. 'You did very well but you're a little too cautious in your forecasts. I *enjoy* risk,' he imparted, watching with amusement as she frowned in surprise at that admission. 'You've got the job. I hope you can take the heat. Not everyone can.'

'If you shout at me, I'll probably shout back,' Merry warned him warily.

And an appreciative grin slashed his shapely lips, making him so powerfully attractive that for a split second she simply stared, unable to look away. 'You may just work out very well.'

So began the most exciting phase of Merry's working life. Merry was the most junior member of Angel's personal staff but the one he always entrusted with figures. Sybil was thrilled by the promotion her niece had won but would have been horrified by the long hours Merry worked and the amount of responsibility she carried.

'The boss has got the hots for you,' one of her male co-workers told her with amusement when she had been two months in the job. 'Obviously you have something all those long tall blondes he parades through here don't, because he's always watching you.'

'I haven't noticed anything,' she said firmly, reluctant to let that kind of comment go unchallenged.

But even as she spoke she knew she was very carefully impersonal and unobtrusive in Angel's vicinity because she was conscious of him in a way she had not been conscious of a man before. If she was foolish enough to risk a head-on collision with his spectacular liquid honey eyes, her tummy somersaulted, her mouth dried and she couldn't catch her breath. Feeling like that mortified her. She knew it was attraction and she didn't like it, not only because he was her boss, but also because it made her feel out of control.

And then fate took a hand when Merry firmly believed that neither of them would ever have made any sort of a move. A highly contagious flu virus had decimated the staff and as his employees fell by the wayside Merry found herself increasingly exposed to working alone with Angel. At the office late one evening, he offered her a drink and a ride home. She said no thanks to the drink, deeming it unwise, and yes to the ride because it would get her home faster.

In the lift on the way down to the underground

car park, Angel studied her with smouldering dark golden eyes. She felt dizzy and hot, as if her clothes were shrink-wrapped to her skin, preventing her from normal breathing. He lifted a long-fingered brown hand and traced his fingertips along the full curve of her lower lip in a caress that left her trembling, and then, as though some invisible line of restraint had snapped inside him, he crushed her back against the mirrored wall and kissed her, hungrily, feverishly, wildly with the kind of passion she was defenceless against.

'Come home with me,' he urged in a raw undertone as she struggled to pull herself back together while the lift doors stood open beside them.

Her flushed face froze. 'Absolutely not. We made a mistake. Let's forget about it.'

'That's not always possible,' Angel breathed thickly. 'I've been trying to forget about the way you make me feel for weeks.'

Disconcerted by that blunt admission as he stepped out of the lift, Merry muttered dismissively, 'That's just sex. Ignore it.'

Angel stared back at her in wonderment. '*Ignore* it?'

As the lift doors began to close with her still inside it, he reached in and held them open. 'Come on.'

'I'll get the Tube as usual.'

'Don't be childish,' Angel ground out. 'I am fully in control.'

Merry wasn't convinced, remembering that mad, exciting grab and the slam of her body back against the lift wall, but that instant of hesitation was her undoing because without hesitation Angel closed a hand over hers and pulled her out of the lift. 'I'll drop you home.'

'There are boundaries that shouldn't be crossed,' she told him with precision on the way to his car.

'Don't preach at me,' Angel sliced back in a driven undertone. 'I don't have a history of making moves on my staff. You are a one-off.'

'And it won't happen again now that we're both on our guard so let's forget about it,' Merry counselled, sliding breathlessly into a long silver low-slung bullet of a vehicle that she suspected was worth many times more than her annual salary. 'I prevented you from making a mistake.'

'You're preaching again,' Angel derided. 'If I hadn't stopped kissing you we'd still be in the lift!'

'No. I would've pushed you away,' she insisted with cool assurance.

She gave him her address, although he didn't seem to need it, and the journey through heavy traffic was silent, tense and unnerving. He pulled up at the kerb outside the ugly building where she lived. 'You could afford to live in a better area than this,' he censured.

'I have a healthy savings account,' she told him with pride, releasing her seat belt at the same time as he reached for her again.

His wide sensual mouth crushed hers with burning hunger and no small amount of frustration. Her whole body leapt as though he had punched a button detonating something deep down inside her, releasing a hot surge of tingling awareness in her pelvis that made her hips squirm and her nipples pinch painfully tight.

Angel lifted his tousled dark head. 'I'm still waiting on you pushing me away. You're all talk and no action,' he condemned.

'I don't think you'd appreciate a slap,' Merry framed frigidly, her face burning with mortification.

'If it meant that you ditched the icy control I'd be begging for it,' Angel husked suggestively, soft and low, the growl of his accent shaking her up.

Merry launched out of his sports car as though jet-propelled, uncharacteristically flustered and shaken that she had failed to live up to her own very high principles on acceptable behaviour. She should've pushed him away, slapped him, thumped him if necessary to drive her message home. Nothing less would cool his heels. He was a highly competitive, aggressive male, who viewed defeat as an ongoing challenge.

His car stayed at the kerb until she stalked into the building and only then did she breathe again, filling her compressed lungs and shivering as though she had stepped out of a freezing snowstorm. She felt all shaken up, shaken up and *stirred* in a way she didn't appreciate and almost hated him for.

The feel of his mouth on hers, the *taste* of it, the explosive charge of heat hurtling at breakneck speed down into her belly and spreading to other, more intimate places she never ever thought about. How dared he do that to her? She would lodge a complaint of sexual harassment! Didn't he know what he was risking? But being Angel, he wouldn't care, wouldn't even stop to consider that he was playing with fire. Indeed, the knowledge would only energise and stimulate him because he loved to push the limits.

She curled up tight in her bed that night, overwhelmed by her first real experience of sexual temptation. When he kissed her she couldn't think, couldn't breathe. A kiss had never had that effect on her before and she was unnerved by the discovery that a kiss could be that influential. She toyed with the idea of complaining about sexual harassment, pictured Angel laughing fearlessly in the

face of such a threat and finally decided that she
didn't want the embarrassment of that on her employment record. Particularly when such a claim
would fail because she hadn't pushed him away,
hadn't given him an immediate rejection.

The next day she was very nervous going into
work, but Angel didn't do or say anything that was
different and she was strangely irritated by that
reality: that he could act as though he had never
offered to take her home to bed for the night and,
afterwards, simply treat her like everyone else.
But those same moments of intimacy had carried
a higher price for *her*. It was as though he had
stripped away her tough outer layer and chipped
her out of her cautious shell to ensure that she
began feeling physical and emotional responses
she had comfortably held at bay until she'd met
him.

During the week that followed she was feverishly aware of Angel to a degree that sent her temperature rocketing. When he looked at her, it was
as if a blast of concentrated heat lit her up inside
and her bra would feel scratchy against her tender nipples and a dull ache would stir between her
thighs, her every tiny reaction in his presence like
a slap in the face that shamed her. It was a terri-
ble destructive wanting that wouldn't go away. He
had lit the spark and she seemed stuck with the

spread of the fire licking away at her nerves and her fierce pride.

At the end of that week, Angel asked her to stay behind after everyone else had left to go for drinks.

'Next on the agenda…*us*,' Angel murmured sibilantly.

Merry shot him a withering appraisal. 'There is no us.'

'Exactly,' Angel pronounced with satisfaction. 'Scratch the itch and it goes away and dies, ignore it and it festers.'

'Your seduction vocabulary needs attention,' Merry quipped, standing straight in front of him, grudging amusement dancing in her crystalline eyes.

Angel grimaced. 'I don't do seduction.'

'I don't do one-night stands.'

'So if I make it dinner and sex I'm in with a chance?' A sardonic ebony brow elevated.

'No chance whatsoever,' Merry contradicted with pleasure. 'I'm a virgin and I'm not trading that for some sleazy night with my boss.'

'A virgin?' Angel was aghast. *'Seriously?'*

'Seriously,' Merry traded without embarrassment, reflecting on how her mother had fallen pregnant with her and determined to make every choice that took her in the opposite direction. 'Sex should mean something more than scratching an itch.'

Angel sprang upright behind his desk, all supple, graceful motion, the fine, expensive fabric of his suit pulling taut over powerful thigh muscles and definable biceps. Her mouth ran dry, her eyes involuntarily clinging to his every movement. 'It's never been anything more for me,' he admitted drily. 'But I take offence at the word "sleazy". I am never sleazy and… I don't do virgins.'

'Good to know,' Merry breathed tightly, watching his shirt ripple ever so slightly over his muscular chest as he exhaled while cursing her intense physical awareness of him. 'May I go home now?'

'I'll drop you back.'

'That's not necessary,' she told him coolly.

'I decide what's necessary around here,' Angel pronounced, throwing the door wide and heading for the lift. 'You realise you're as rare as a unicorn in my world? Are you holding out for marriage?'

Involuntarily amused by his curiosity, Merry laughed. 'Of course not. I'm just waiting for something *real*. I'm not a fan of casual or meaningless.'

Angel lounged back fluidly against the wall of the lift, all naked predator and jungle grace. 'I'm casual but I'm very real,' he told her huskily, his deep dark drawl roughening and trickling down her taut spine like a spectral caress.

'Oh, switch it off,' Merry groaned. 'We're like salt and pepper except you can't mix us.'

'Because you've got too many rules, too many barriers. Why is that?'

'Like you are actually interested?' Merry jibed.

'I *am* interested,' Angel growled, dark golden eyes flashing as the lift doors sprang back. 'I want you.'

'Only because you can't have me,' Merry interposed drily, her skin coming up in gooseflesh as he flashed her a ferocious appraisal capable of flaying her skin from her bones. 'That's how basic you are.'

'You're becoming rude.'

'Your persistence is making me rude,' Merry told him.

'I want to see your hair loose,' Angel bit out impatiently. 'It's unusually long.'

'My mother kept on cutting it short when I was little because it was easier to look after. Now I grow it because I can,' she said truthfully, her stomach flipping as he shot a sudden charismatic smile at her, his lean, darkly beautiful face vibrant with amusement.

'You're a control freak,' he breathed lazily. 'Takes one to know one, *glikia mou.*'

'That's why we don't get on,' Merry pointed out.

'We don't get on because you have a very annoying sort of pious vibe going,' Angel contradicted. 'You're smug.'

'No, I'm not,' she argued instantly as they crossed the half-empty car park.

'You think you're superior to me because you're not at the mercy of your hormones…but you *were* when I touched you,' Angel breathed, caging her in against the passenger door of his car, the heat of his lean, powerful body perceptible even through the inches separating them and the rich, evocative scent of husky male and exotic cologne filling her nostrils. His hands braced either side of her, not actually touching her quivering length, and her knees turned weak at the thought that he *might* touch her. 'You can hardly breathe when I'm this close to you. I *see* that, I *know* that…every time I try to step back, it sucks me back in.'

He was like an impenetrable force field surrounding her. She knew she could push him away, she knew he wouldn't fight, she knew he wouldn't do anything she didn't want him to do and a weird sense of unexpected power engulfed her. He was still coming back at her because he couldn't resist the pull between them and she couldn't resist it either. It was a weakness deep down inside her that she couldn't suppress. Nobody had ever made her feel the way he was making her feel and that was a thrill on its own, a shot of adrenalin in her veins to match the feverish pound of her heartbeat. She wanted him. The knowledge ploughed through her like a battering ram, casting everything she had thought she knew about herself into a broken jumble of messy pieces.

'You're not my type,' she whispered in dry-mouthed protest.

'You're not my type either,' Angel admitted thickly. 'But I'd still have sex in a car park with you any time you cared to ask.'

'Not about to ask,' Merry confided shakily. 'Take me home…back off.'

'You're making a major production of this again,' Angel accused, flashing his key fob to open the car. 'Stop doing that. It's…it's bizarrely unnerving.'

She climbed into his car in a daze, the throb between her legs angry and unsettling, the sensual smoulder in the air almost unbearable, every nerve ending painfully aware of it. She didn't know how he did that using only words and looks. It was terrifying. He had wiped her mind clean, made her feel stuff she didn't want to feel, rocked the foundations of her security.

'I don't like you,' she admitted.

'*Thee mou*…you don't have to like me, you only have to want me…and you do.'

And it was agonisingly true, she registered in dismay. Her brain didn't seem to have anything to do with the equation. She thoroughly disapproved of everything he was and yet the chemistry between them was wild and dominant.

'We have one night together and sate the craving. Then we put it away and bury it,' Angel intoned in a driven undertone.

'I thought you didn't do virgins.'

'Evidently you were born to be my single exception.'

'Is this an actual negotiation?' Merry enquired incredulously.

'We have to sort this out. You're taking my mind off work,' Angel complained. 'I can't handle watching you all day and fantasising about you all night. It's bad for business.'

'What's in it for me?' Merry whispered unevenly.

'I'm superlative at sex.'

'Oh…' Her lashes fluttered, her tummy somersaulting again as she wondered if she really was about to do what he wanted her to do, what *she* herself wanted to do. And that was the answer there and then when she was least expecting to see or understand it.

He would make a great introduction to sex for her, she thought dizzily. It would end the insane craving he had awakened inside her and maybe then she could return to her normal tranquil self. That prospect had huge appeal for her. The need would be satisfied, the intolerable longing ended. All right, it wasn't the big romance with hearts and flowers that she had dimly envisioned, but then possibly that had never been a very practical aspiration. What he was offering was basic and honest even if it was casual and uncommitted and everything she had once sworn she would never participate in. It was not as though she had been saving herself for a wedding ring. She had been saving herself for love, but love hadn't happened.

'So, you're suggesting that I just use you,' Merry remarked grittily as he pulled into another underground car park.

'We use each other,' Angel exhaled in a rush and, killing the engine, stretched out a long powerful arm to enclose her in almost the same moment.

His mouth crashed down on hers with a hunger that blew her away. Somehow he made it that she didn't remember getting out of the car, didn't remember getting into a lift or emerging from it. There was only that insane, greedy melding of their mouths and the frantic impatient activity of their hands in a dimly lit hall. Her coat fell off or maybe he helped it. His jacket disappeared at similar speed. She kicked off her shoes. He wrenched off his tie and cannoned into a door as he lifted her off her feet.

'We have to slow down,' he told her roughly,

dark golden eyes shimmering like gold ingots, his
sexual excitement patent. 'Or I'll screw this up
for you.'

He laid her down on a wide, comfortable mattress and stood over her, stripping without inhibition. All she wanted was his mouth on hers again,
that magical escape from the limits of her own
body that sent her flying higher than she had ever
known she could fly. He shed his trousers and her
attention locked warily on the very obvious bulge
in his boxers while she struggled to accept that she
could, even briefly, be with a man who was chroni-
cally untidy and dropped clothes in a heap on the
floor. Not her type, not her type; she rhymed it like
a mantra inside her head, her bulwark against getting attached in any way. It was sex and she didn't
want to regard it as anything else.

He unzipped her dress and flipped her over to
remove it with deft precision and release her bra,
before pausing to carefully unsnap the clasp in her
hair and let his skilled mouth roam across her pale
shoulders. He tugged her round and up to him then,
long fingers lifting to feather her curtain of dark
coffee-coloured hair round her shoulders, thready
shimmers of lighter caramel appearing in the light
filtering in from the hall.

'You have amazing hair,' he muttered intently,
gazing down into blue eyes as pale as an Arctic sky.

'Is that a fetish of yours?'

'Not that I've noticed, but that prissy little smile of yours turns me on no end,' Angel confided, disconcerting her.

'I do *not* have a prissy smile.'

'Talking too much,' Angel growled, crushing her ripe mouth beneath his again, running his hands down the sides of her narrow ribcage to dispose of her bra and let his hands rise to cup the small delicate mounds of her breasts.

As his thumbs grazed her sensitive nipples a gasp parted Merry's lips, and when his hungry mouth followed there she fell back against the pillows and dug her fingers into his thick tangle of curls. Heat arrowed in stormy flashes right to her core, leaving her insanely conscious of how excited she was becoming. Her thighs pressed together, her hips dug into the mattress as she struggled to get a grip on herself, but it was as if her body were streaking ahead of her and no matter how hard she tried to catch it, she couldn't.

He shifted position, ran his tongue down over her straining midriff to her navel, parted her from her knickers without her noticing, traced her inner thighs with a devil's expertise until she was splayed out like a sacrifice. And then the flood of crazy pleasure came at her in breathless, jolting stabs that shocked and roused her to a level that was almost unbearable. She was shaken by what she was allowing him to do and how much her body craved it and how very little she could control her own reactions. She twisted and turned, hauled him back to her at one point and kissed him breathless, wanting, needing, trembling on the edge of something she didn't understand.

The tight bands in her pelvis strained to hold in the wild searing shots of pleasure gripping her and then her control broke and she writhed in a wild frenzy of release. The sound of her own gasping cry startled her, her eyes flying wide, and Angel grinned shamelessly down at her like a very sexy pirate, a dark shadow of stubble merely accentuating his fantastic bone structure.

'You're staying the whole night,' he told her thickly.

'No,' Merry muttered, head rolling back on the pillows as he crawled up her body like the predator he truly was. 'Once it's done, it's over.'

'You are so stubborn,' Angel groaned in frustration, nipping up her slender throat to find her swollen lips again, teasing and tasting and letting his tongue plunge and twin with hers until she was beyond thought and argument again. He donned protection.

He eased into her slowly, very slowly, and impatience assailed her. She didn't want or need to be treated like fine china that might shatter or like that rare unicorn he had mentioned. Her body was slick and eager again, the pulse at the heart of her racing with anticipation. She tilted under him, angling up her hips, and the invitation was too much for his control and he jerked over her and plunged deep. A brief burning sting of pain made her stiffen and gasp.

'That's your own fault,' Angel growled in exasperation. 'If you would just lie still.'

'I'm not a blow-up doll.'

'I was trying not to hurt you.'

'I'm not breakable either,' Merry argued, every skin cell on red alert as she felt her body slowly stretch to enclose his, tiny little shimmers of exquisite sensation flying through her as he began to move, hinting that the best was yet to come. 'Don't stop.'

And he didn't. He sank deep into her with a shuddering groan of pleasure and the pace picked up, jolting her with waves of glorious excitement. She arched her body up, suddenly needy again, hungry again, marvelling at the limitless capacity of her body to feel more and yet more. But this time the climb to pleasure was slower and she writhed, blue eyes lighting up with impatience and a need she had never expressed before. Her heart raced, her pulses pounded and that sweet,

seductive throb of delight grew and grew inside
her until she could contain it no longer. Every barrier dropped as her body exploded into an ecstatic
climax that left her limp and stunned.

Angel released her from his weight but made a
move to pull her under his arm and retain a hold
on her. Quick as a flash Merry evaded him, her
whole being bent on immediate escape. They had
had sex but she didn't want to hang around for the
aftermath. Dignity, she told herself staunchly, dic-
tated an immediate departure. She slid out of the
other side of the bed, bending down to scoop up
her discarded clothes.

'I asked you to stay,' Angel reminded her.

'I'm going home,' she said as he vaulted out
of bed and headed into what she presumed was
a bathroom, his lean, powerful body emanating
impatience and annoyance in perceptible waves.

She would have liked a shower but she was determined not to linger. With a grimace, she pulled
her clothes back on and was out in the hall cram-
ming her feet back into her shoes and hurriedly
calling a taxi when Angel reappeared, bronzed and
still unashamedly naked in the bedroom doorway.
'I don't want you to leave.'

'I've already ordered a taxi.' Merry tilted her
chin, her long hair streaming untidily round her

flushed heart-shaped face. 'We agreed and it's better like this.'

'I asked for one night—'

'You can't have everything your way,' Merry declared flatly. 'I enjoyed myself but all good things come to an end.'

Angel swore in Greek. 'You drive me insane.'

'What's your problem? According to your forecast, we're done and dusted now,' she pointed out helplessly.

Yet for all her proud nonchalance in front of him, Merry travelled home in a daze of mounting panic. Back at her apartment she had to wait until the shower was free. She felt shell-shocked by what she had done. Her body ached but her brain ached almost as much, trying to rationalise the fleeting madness that had overtaken her. She tried to examine it from Angel's unemotional point of view, but that didn't work for her when her own emotions were throwing tantrums and storming about inside her as much as if she had killed someone. *Done and dusted, forget about it now,* she reminded herself doggedly. He had much more experience in such encounters than she had, had to know what he was talking about. The curiosity and that unnatural hunger had been satisfied and now it would all die a natural death and become an embarrassing memory that she'd never ever share with anyone, she told herself with determination.

Only in the days that followed Merry slowly came to appreciate that, for all his evident experience, Angel Valtinos had got it badly wrong. Feed a cold, starve a fever was a saying she had grown up with, and before very long had passed she knew that it had been a serious mistake to *feed* the fever. She saw it in the way Angel's stunning dark eyes locked on her like magnets, heard it in the terseness of his instructions to her and she felt the pull of him inside herself as if he had attached a secret chain to her. Excitement crashed over her when he was close by, her temperature climbing, her heart thumping. Slowly, painfully, she came to appreciate that she was infatuated with him and very nearly as giddy and mindless as a silly schoolgirl in his vicinity. The suspicion that she was more her mother's daughter than she had ever dreamt she could be appalled her.

Was that the real explanation of why she had slept with Angel Valtinos? She had asked herself again and again why she had done that, why she had made such an impulsive decision that went against everything she believed, and now she was being faced with an answer that she loathed. At some point in their relationship she had begun getting attached to him, possibly around the time she had started admiring his intellect and shrewd business instincts. That attachment was pitiful, she decided with angry self-loathing, and in haste she began to look for another job, desperate to leave Angel and Valtinos Enterprises behind her.

Two weeks after their first encounter, Angel showed up at her apartment one evening without the smallest warning. The same angry frustration that powered him was running through her.

'What are you doing here?' she demanded, far from pleased to be surprised in her cotton pyjamas, fresh from the shower and bare of make-up.

Angel grimaced, his lean, darkly handsome features taut and troubled as he leant back against her bedroom door to close it. 'My car brought me here.'

'What on earth—?' she began, disconcerted by his sudden appearance in a place where she had never imagined seeing him.

Angel settled volatile dark golden eyes on her angrily. 'I *can't* stay away,' he grated rawly, his beautiful mouth compressing.

'B-but…we agreed,' she stammered.

'Massive fail,' Angel framed darkly. 'Biggest bloody mistake of my life!'

Merry almost laughed and fortunately killed the urge. It was simply that Angel's innate love of drama not only amused her, but somehow touched

her somewhere down deep inside, somewhere
where she was soft and emotional and vulnerable
even though she didn't want to be. He had come to
her even though he didn't want to. He resented his
desire for her, had tried to stamp it out and failed.
She grasped immediately that that weakness for
her infuriated him.

'I want to be with you tonight.'

'Angel—'

He came down on the bed beside her and framed
her face with long, cool brown fingers. 'Say my
name again,' he demanded.

'No,' she said stubbornly. 'I don't do what you
tell me to do outside working hours.'

'*Thee mou*...stop challenging me,' he groaned,
tilting her head back to follow the long, elegant
column of her throat down to the slope of her
shoulder, nipping and kissing a tantalising path
across her sensitised skin while she quivered. 'This
isn't me. This isn't what I'm about.'

'Then why are you here?' she whispered weakly.

'Can't stay away.' He carried her hand down
to where he was hot and hard and wanting and
groaned without inhibition as she stroked him
through the fine, crisp fabric of his well-cut trousers.

Heat coursed through her in molten waves, the
hunger unleashed afresh. Simply touching him in-

flamed her. She tried to fight it, she tried to fasten it down and ground herself, but Angel smashed any hope of control by welding dark golden eyes to hers and kissing her with barely contained ferocity. Not a single thought passed her mind beyond the thrillingly obvious reality that he needed her and couldn't stay away. That knowledge vanquished every other consideration. She kissed him back with the same uncontrollable, desperate passion.

'I intended to take you out to dinner,' Angel admitted breathlessly as he fought with her pyjamas, his sleek, deft skills with feminine clothing deserting him.

'You hungry?' she gasped, almost strangling him with his own tie in her struggle to loosen it.

'Only for you,' he growled fiercely against her swollen mouth. 'Watching you round the office all day, being unable to touch, even to look.'

And then they were naked in her bed, naked and frantic and so tormentingly hungry for each other that she writhed and squirmed and he fought to hold her still. He produced a condom, tore it from the wrapper with his teeth. 'We don't want an accident,' he said unevenly.

'No, no accidents,' she agreed helplessly, lying there, shocked by what she was doing but participating all the same, quite unable to deny him. Their clothes lay festooned all around them and she didn't care. Angel had come to her and she was happy about that, there in her pin-neat room made messy by his presence.

He drove into her yielding flesh with a heart-felt sound of satisfaction and she wrapped her legs round him, arching up and gasping at every fluid stroke. The excitement heightened exponentially, the pulsing pound of intolerable desire driving them off the edge fast into a hot, sweaty tangle of limbs and shuddering fulfilment.

Angel pressed his sensual mouth against her brow and eased back, only to grate out a curse in Greek. 'I broke the condom!' he growled in harried explanation as she stared up at him, recognising the stress and anxiety in his expressive gaze.

As if a simultaneous alarm bell had sounded, Angel flipped back from her and slid fluidly out of bed while Merry hurriedly hid her fast-cooling body under the duvet they had lain on. Her eyes were wide with consternation.

'This has never happened to me before,' Angel assured her, hastily getting back into his clothes.

Merry pondered the idea of mentioning that dinner invite and discarded it again. She had nothing comforting to say to him, nothing likely to improve his mood. She wasn't on the pill, wasn't taking any contraceptive precautions, a reality that now made her feel very foolish. Why hadn't she rethought her outlook the minute she'd ended up in bed with Angel Valtinos? Wasn't a woman supposed to look after herself?

'I'm not on anything,' she admitted reluctantly.

Angel dug out his wallet and flipped out a card. 'Come in late tomorrow. See this doctor first. He's a friend of mine. He'll check you out,' he told her, setting the card down by the bed.

And within a minute he was gone. *Wham-bam— no, thank you, ma'am,* she acknowledged with a sinking heart and a strong need for a shower.

If only she could shower the thoughts out of her head and the feelings in her heart as easily, she concluded wretchedly. She felt sick, humiliated and rejected. She also hated herself. A contraceptive accident had sent Angel into a nosedive, his horror unconcealed. Did she hold that against him when trepidation had seized her by the throat as well?

But luckily, that night she had no grasp at all of the nightmare that was waiting to unfold and the many months of unhappiness that would follow as punishment for her irresponsibility. In effect, she was still a complete innocent then. She was hopelessly infatuated with a man who only lusted after her and with a lust that died the instant a condom failed. That was why she had held herself back from casual sex, seeking the feelings and the certain amount of safety that came with them…

Her first wake-up call to what she was truly dealing with came early the next morning. She went, as instructed, to see the suave private doctor, who ran a battery of tests on her and then casually offered her the morning-after pill. She didn't want it, hadn't ever even thought about whether or not she approved of that option, but when it was suggested to her, it grated on her, and even though she could see the doctor's surprise at her refusal she saw no reason to explain her attitude. Had such a possibility been available to her mother, she reckoned that she herself would never have been born and that was a sobering acknowledgement. Had Angel sent her to that doctor quite deliberately to ensure that she was offered that option? She planned to have that out with him the instant she got a moment alone with him.

Unfortunately what she didn't know then was that it would be many, many weeks before she had the opportunity of a moment alone with Angel again and even then she only finally achieved that meeting by stalking him to one of his regular retreats.

When she finally arrived at work after seeing the doctor she was sent straight into one of the meeting rooms where a senior HR person and a company lawyer awaited her. There she was presented with a compromise agreement by which, in return for substantial compensation, she would immediately cease working for Valtinos Enterprises and leave without disclosing her reasons for doing so to anyone.

The shock and humiliation of that meeting marked Merry long after the event. As soon as she realised that Angel wanted her out of the building and away from him, no matter what it cost him, she felt sick inside. Had he assumed that she would make a nuisance of herself in some way? His ruthless rejection and instant dismissal of what they had briefly shared shook her rigid and taught her a hard lesson. Angel always put himself first and evidently her continued presence at the office would make him uncomfortable. That she did not deserve such harsh treatment didn't come into it for him.

In disgust and mortification Merry took the money she was offered because she felt she had no better alternative and she had to live until she found another job. But that was the day the first seed of her hatred had been sown...

CHAPTER THREE

'FERGUS ASKED ME where he should take you tomor-row,' Sybil volunteered, shooting Merry straight back into the present with that surprising an-nouncement. 'I thought that was a bit wet of him. I mean, doesn't he have any ideas of his own? But obviously he wants you to enjoy yourself.'

A bit wet sounded all right to Merry, who was still reeling from the consequences of Angel's me-me-me approach to life. A macho, self-assured man was hugely impressive and sexy only until he turned against you and became an enemy, armed to the teeth with legal sharks.

'I suggested a trip to the seaside for you and Elyssa. I know you love the beach,' Sybil mused. 'Fergus does like children.'

'Yes,' Merry agreed quietly, scooping Elyssa off the older woman's lap to feed her while wonder-ing what it would have been like to have a father for her daughter. Would he have helped out with their child? Taken a real interest? She suppressed the thought, knowing it probably came from the reality that *she* had had to grow up without a father. She had, however, visited her father once, but his enraged betrayed wife had been present as well and the visit had been a disaster. Her father had only asked to see her on that one occasion and then never again.

The next morning, Merry finished drying her hair and took the time to apply a little make-up because Elyssa was having her morning nap. Pulling on skinny jeans and a vibrant cerise tee, she dug her feet into comfy shoes. She was heading downstairs again with Elyssa anchored on her hip when the phone rang. Breathless, she tucked it under her chin while she lowered her daughter to the hearth rug.

'Yes?'

'I'm in the office,' her aunt told her curtly. 'Elyssa's father is here demanding to see her. I'll keep him here with me until you come.'

Shock and disbelief engulfed Merry in a dizzy tide. She snatched Elyssa back off the rug and wondered frantically what to do with her daughter while she dealt with Angel, because she didn't want him to see her. Her mind was a chaotic blur because she couldn't imagine Angel travelling down to Suffolk just to see the child he had once done everything possible to avoid and deny. It was true that since he had been informed of Elyssa's birth he had made repeated requests to meet his daughter, but Merry had seen no good reason to cater to his natural human curiosity and she herself wanted nothing more to do with him.

After all, as soon as Angel had learned that she was pregnant he had brought his lawyers in to handle everything. They had drawn up a legal agreement by which Merry was paid a ridiculous amount of money every month but only for as long as she kept quiet about her daughter's parentage. Merry currently paid the money into a trust she had set up for Elyssa's future, reckoning that that was the best she could do for her daughter.

She left the cottage with Elyssa tucked into her well-padded pushchair, her toy bunny clutched between her fingers. Walking into the rescue centre, she saw a long black limousine sitting parked and she swallowed hard at the sight of it. Angel didn't flaunt the Valtinos wealth but even at the office she had seen occasional glimpses of a world and lifestyle far different from her own. He wore diamond cufflinks and his shirts had monograms embroidered on the pockets. Every garment he wore was tailored by hand at great expense and he thought nothing of it because from birth he had never known anything else.

She pushed the buggy into the barn, where the kennel staff hung out when they took a break. 'Will you watch Elyssa for me for ten minutes?' she asked anxiously of the three young women, chattering over mugs of coffee.

'Can we take her out of the pram and play with her?' one of them pressed hopefully.

A smile softened Merry's troubled face. 'Of course...' she agreed, hastening out again to head for the rescue centre office.

What on earth was Angel doing here? And how could she face him when the very idea of facing him again made her feel queasy with bad memories? They had last met the day she'd tracked him down to tell him that she was pregnant. Those liquid-honey eyes had turned black-diamond hard, his shock and distaste stark as a banner.

'Do you want it?' he had asked doubtingly, earning her hatred with every syllable of that leading question. 'Scratch that. It was politically incorrect. Naturally I will support you in whatever choice you make.'

How could she come back from that punishing recollection and act normally? She thought of Elyssa's innocent sweetness and the reality that her father didn't want her, had *never* wanted her, and the knowledge hurt Merry, making her wonder if her own father had felt the same about her. Even worse, she was convinced that allowing any kind of contact between father and daughter would only result in Elyssa getting hurt at some later stage. In her opinion, Angel was too selfish and too spoiled to be a caring or committed parent.

As she rounded the corner of the tiny office building a startling scene met her eyes. Poised outside the door, Sybil had her shotgun aimed at Angel, who was predictably lounging back against the wall of the kennels opposite as though he had not a care in the world.

'Will you call this madwoman off me?' Angel demanded with derisive sibilance when he heard her footsteps and without turning his arrogant dark head. 'She won't let me move.'

'It's all right, Sybil,' Merry said tautly. 'Elyssa is in the barn.'

Angel's arrogant dark head flipped, the long, predatory power of his lean, strong body suddenly rippling with bristling tension. 'What's my daughter doing in a barn? And who's looking after her?' he demanded in a driven growl.

Sybil lowered her shotgun and broke it open to safely extract the cartridges. 'I'll take her back home with me,' she declared, entirely ignoring Angel.

'Come into the office and we'll talk,' Merry framed coldly as his dark eyes locked on her tense face.

'I'm not very good at talking,' Angel acknowledged without embarrassment as he straightened. 'That's why I use lawyers.'

In an angry defensive movement, Merry thrust wide the door of the little office before spinning back round to say, 'What the hell are you doing here?'

'I warned you that I intended to visit,' Angel bit out impatiently.

Merry thought about the letter she had bottled out of opening and uneasily looked at him for the first time in months. The sheer power of his volatile presence made her tummy turn hollow and her legs wobble. He was still so wickedly beautiful that he made her teeth clench with fierce resentment. It wasn't fair that he should look so untouched by all that had passed between them, that he should stand there perfectly at his ease and glossily well groomed, sheathed in his elegant charcoal-grey designer suit. It was especially unfair that he should still have the nerve to voice a demand for a right he had surrendered entirely of his own volition before their daughter was even born. 'And I've already told your lawyers that I won't accept *any* kind of visit from you!'

'I won't accept that, not even if I have to spend the rest of my life and yours fighting you.' Angel mapped those boundaries for her, wanting her to know that there would be no escape from his demands until he got what he wanted. He would not accept defeat, regardless of what it cost him. He had lost his father's respect and he was determined to retrieve it and get to know his child.

Frowning, black brows lowering, he studied Merry, incredulous at her continuing defiance while marvelling at the quiet inner strength he sensed in her, which he had never noticed in a woman before. She had cut her hair, which now fell in glossy abundance to just below her shoulders. He was ridiculously disappointed by that fashion update. There had been something ultra-feminine about that unusually long hair that he had liked. She was also thinner than she had been and there had not been much of her to begin with, he conceded reflectively. She looked like a teenager with her long, coltish legs outlined by distressed denim and with her rounded little breasts pushing at the cotton of her top so that he could see the prominent points of her lush nipples. He went hard and gritted his teeth, furious with himself for that weakness but... *Thee mou*, shorn of her conservative office apparel, she looked ridiculously sexy.

'Why can't you simply move on from this and

forget we exist?' Merry demanded in fierce frustration. 'A year ago, that's what you wanted and I gave it to you. I signed everything your legal team put in front of me. You didn't want to be a father. You didn't want to know anything about her and you didn't want her associated with your precious name. What suddenly changed?'

Angel's lean, hard jaw line took on an aggressive slant. 'Maybe I've changed,' he admitted, sharply disconcerting her.

Merry's tense face stiffened with suspicion. 'That's doubtful. You are what you are.'

'Everyone is capable of change and sometimes change simply happens whether you want it to or not,' Angel traded, his lean, dark features taut. 'When you first told me that you were pregnant a year ago, I didn't think through what I was doing. Gut instinct urged me to protect my way of life. I listened to my lawyers, took their advice and now we've got…now we've got an intolerable mess.'

Merry forced herself to breathe in deep and slow and stay calm. He sounded sincere but she didn't trust him. 'It's the way you made it and now you have to live with it.'

Angel threw back his broad shoulders and lifted his arrogant dark head high, effortlessly dominating the small cluttered room. Even though Merry was a comfortable five feet eight inches tall, he was well over six feet in height and stood the tall-est in most gatherings. 'I can't live with it,' he told her with flat finality. 'I *will* continue to fight for access to my daughter.'

The breath fluttered in Merry's drying throat, consternation and fury punching up through her, bringing a flood of emotion with it. 'I *hate* you, Angel! If you make any more threats, if you bombard me with more legal letters, I will hate you even more! When is enough *enough*?' she hurled at him with bitter emphasis.

'When I can finally establish a normal relation-ship with my daughter,' Angel responded, his lean, strong face set with stubborn resolve. 'It is my duty to establish that relationship and I won't shirk it.'

'The way you shirked everything else that went with fatherhood?' Merry scorned. 'The responsi-bility? The commitment? The caring? I was just a pregnant problem you threw money at!'

'I won't apologise for that. I was raised to solve problems that way,' Angel admitted grittily. 'I was taught to put my faith in lawyers and to protect myself first.'

'Angel…you are strong enough to protect your-self in a cage full of lions!' Merry shot back at him wrathfully. 'You didn't *need* the lawyers when I wasn't making any demands!'

A ton of hurt and turbulent emotion was sucking Merry down but she fought it valiantly. She was trying so hard not to throw pointless recriminations at him. In an effort to put a physical barrier between them she flopped down in the chair behind the desk. 'Did you ever…even once…think about *feelings*?' she prompted involuntarily.

Angel frowned at her, wondering what she truly wanted from him, wondering how much he would be willing to give in return for access to his daughter. It wasn't a calculation he wanted to do at that moment, not when she was sitting there, shoulders rigid, heart-shaped face stiff and pale as death. 'Feelings?' he repeated blankly.

'My feelings,' Merry specified helplessly. 'How it would feel for me to sleep with a man one night and go into work the next day and realise that he couldn't even stand to have me stay in the same building to do my job?'

Angel froze as if she had fired an ice gun at him, colour receding beneath his bronzed skin, his gorgeous dark eyes suddenly screened by his ridiculously luxuriant black lashes. 'No, I can't say I did. I didn't view it in that light,' he admitted curtly. 'I thought separation was the best thing for both of us because our relationship had crossed too many boundaries and got out of hand. I also ensured that your career prospects were not damaged in any way.'

Merry closed her eyes tight, refusing to look at him any longer. He had once told her that he didn't do virgins and it seemed that he didn't do feelings either. He was incapable of putting himself in her shoes and imagining how she had felt. 'I felt... absolutely mortified that day, completely humiliated, *hurt*,' she spelt out defiantly. 'The money didn't soften the blow and I only took it because I didn't know how long it would take for me to find another job.'

Angel saw pain in her pale blue eyes and heard the emotion in her roughened voice. Her honesty unnerved him, flayed off a whole layer of protective skin, and he didn't like how it made him feel. 'I had no desire to hurt you, there *was* no such intent,' he countered tautly. 'I realised that our situation had become untenable and in that line I was guiltier than you because I made all the running.'

It was an acknowledgement of fault that would once have softened her. He had created that untenable situation and brutally ditched her when he had had enough of it but his admission didn't come anywhere near soothing the tight ball of hurt in her belly. 'You could have talked to me personally,' she pointed out, refusing to drop the subject.

'I've never talked about stuff like that. I wouldn't know where to begin,' Angel confessed grimly.

'Well, how could you possibly forge a worthwhile bond with a daughter, then?' Merry pressed. 'The minute she annoys you or offends you will you turn your back on her the way you turned your back on me?'

Angel flashed her a seethingly angry appraisal. 'Not for one minute have you and that baby been out of my mind since the day you told me you were pregnant! I did not turn my back on you. I made proper provision for both of you.'

'Yeah, you threw money at us to keep us at a safe distance, yet now here you are breaking your own rules,' Merry whispered shakily.

'What is the point of us wrangling like this?' Angel questioned with rank impatience. 'This is no longer about you and I. This involves a third person with rights of her own even if she is still only a baby. Will you allow me to meet my daughter this afternoon?'

'Apart from everything else—like it being immaterial to you that I hate and distrust you,' Merry framed with thin restraint, 'today's out of the question. I've got a date this afternoon and we're going out.'

Angel tensed, long, powerful muscles pulling taut. He could not explain why he was shocked by the idea of her having a date. Maybe he had been guilty of assuming that she was too busy being a mother at present to worry about enjoying a social life. But the concept of her enjoying herself with another man inexplicably outraged and infuriated him and the vision of her bedding another man when he had been the first, the *only*, made him want to smash something.

His lean brown hands clenched into fists. 'A date?' he queried as jaggedly as if he had a piece of glass in his throat.

Merry stood up behind the desk and squared her slim shoulders. 'Yes, he's taking us to the beach. You have a problem with that as well?'

Us? The realisation that another man, some random, unknown stranger, had access to his daughter when he did not heaped coals of fire on Angel's proud head. He snatched in a stark breath, fighting with all his might to cage his hot temper and his bitterness. 'Yes, I do. Can't you leave her with your aunt and grant me even ten minutes with my own child?' he demanded rawly.

'I'm afraid there isn't time today.' Merry swallowed the lump in her throat, that reminder that Elyssa had rights of her own still filtering back through her like a storm warning, making her appreciate that every decision she made now would have to be explained and defended to satisfy her daughter's questions some years down the road. And just how mean could she afford to be to Angel before her daughter would question her attitude? Question whether her mother had given her daughter's personal needs sufficient weight and importance? Her tummy dive-bombed, her former conviction that she was totally in the right taking a massive dent.

Nobody was ever totally in the right, she reminded herself reluctantly. There were always two sides to every story, every conflict. She was letting herself be influenced by her own feelings, not looking towards the future when Elyssa would demand answers to certain tough questions relating to her father. And did she really want to put herself in the position of having refused to allow her daughter's flesh and blood to even *see* her? Dully it dawned on her that that could well be a step too far in hostilities. Angel had hurt *her*, but that was not indisputable proof that he would hurt his daughter.

'Pick another day this week,' she invited him stiffly, watching surprise and comprehension leap like golden flames into his vivid eyes. 'But you make your arrangements with me, not through your lawyers. You visit for an hour. Let's not raise the bar too high, let's keep it simple. I won't let you take her out anywhere without me and I don't want you arriving with some fancy nanny in tow.'

His dramatic dark eyes shone bright, a tiny

muscle jerking taut at the corner of his wide, sensual mouth. He swung away, momentarily turning his back on her before swinging back and nodding sombrely in agreement with her strictures. But in those revealing few seconds she had recognised the stormy flare of anticipation in his stunning gaze, finally registering that he *had* been serious in his approach and that he did genuinely want to meet his infant daughter.

'Tomorrow morning, then,' Angel pronounced decisively. 'We'll take it from there.'

Take what from where? she almost questioned but she ducked it, worn out by the sheer stress of dealing with him. Inside herself she was trembling with the strain of standing straight and unafraid and hiding her fearful anxiety from him because she knew that Angel would pounce on weakness like a shark catching the scent of blood. 'About ten,' she suggested carefully. 'I have someone to see at half eleven.'

Angel gritted his even white teeth, wanting to ask if she was seeing the boyfriend again, but he had no intention of being foolish enough to ask questions he had no right to demand answers to. She had been under covert surveillance for weeks and he would soon identify the boyfriend from the records he had yet to examine. His mouth quirked because he knew she would be outraged if she knew he was paying a private firm to watch her every move.

But, when it came to protecting a member of the Valtinos family, Angel had no inhibitions. Hired security was as much a part of his life as it was for his mother. Safety came first and his daughter would be at risk of kidnapping were anyone to work out who had fathered her. It was his duty to safeguard his child and he would not apologise for the necessity.

Merry opened the office door to urge him out and followed him to where the limousine sat parked. 'I live in the cottage at the front gate,' she informed him.

'I thought you lived with your aunt,' Angel admitted with a frown.

'When I became a mother I thought it was time for us to get our own space. Sybil practically raised me. I didn't want her to feel that she had to do the same for my daughter,' Merry confided ruefully.

In the summer sunlight she studied Angel's lean, strong face, marvelling at the sleek symmetry of the hard cheekbones and hollows that enhanced his very masculine features. He was a literal work of art. It was little wonder that she had overreacted to his interest and refused to accept how shallow that interest was, she told herself squarely, struggling to calm the stabs of worry that erupted at the prospect of having any further dealings with him.

She would cope. She *had* to cope. So far she had contrived to cope with everything Angel Valtinos had thrown at her, she reminded herself with pride. As long as she remembered who and what he was, she would be fine…wouldn't she?

CHAPTER FOUR

'LETTING ELYSSA'S FATHER visit is the right way to go,' Fergus opined, scrutinising her troubled face with concern before turning to gaze out to sea. 'He treated you badly but that doesn't automatically mean he'll be a bad father. Only time will answer that.'

Merry went pink. As Fergus had combined picking her up with an examination of the latest arrival at the rescue centre, he had heard about the fuss created by Angel's visit earlier in the day and had naturally asked her about it. She looked up at Fergus, drawn by his calm and acceptance of her situation, wondering if it was possible to feel anything or even trust a man again. Fergus stood about an inch under six feet. He had cropped brown hair and cheerful blue eyes and she had never heard him so much as raise his voice while she had already witnessed his compassion and regret when he was treating abused animals.

'Are you over him?' Fergus asked her bluntly.

Merry vented a shaken laugh. 'I certainly hope so.'

And then he kissed her, wrapping her close in the sea breeze, and she froze only momentarily in surprise. Suddenly she found herself wanting to feel more than she actually felt because he was a good guy, ostensibly straightforward and as different from Angel as day was to night. Angel was all twists and turns, dark corners and unpredictability and she had never had any genuine hope of a future with him. Furthermore, Angel had never been her type. He wasn't steady or open or even ready to settle down with conventional expectations. Feelings were foreign and threatening to Angel yet he bristled with untamed emotion. As Fergus freed her mouth and kept an arm anchored to her spine she realised in horror-stricken dismay that she'd spent their entire kiss thinking about Angel and her face burned in shame and discomfiture.

Angel sat in his limo and perused the photo that had been sent to his phone while he angrily wondered if he was a masochist or, indeed, developing sad stalker tendencies. But no, he had to deal with the situation as it was, not as he would've preferred it to be. Even worse, Merry had just upped the stakes, ensuring that Angel had now to raise his game. He wanted to stalk down to that beach and beat the hell out of the opposition. Because that was what Fergus Wickham was: opposition, *serious* opposition.

And naturally, Angel was confident that he was not jealous. After all, with only one exception, he had never experienced jealousy. He had, however, once cherished a singularly pathetic desire for his mother to take as much of an interest in him as she took in her toy boys. He *had* only been about seven years old at the time, he reminded himself forgivingly, and a distinctly naïve child, fondly expecting that, his having spent all term at boarding school, his mother would make him the centre of her loving attention when he finally came home.

Well, he wasn't that naïve now, Angel acknowledged grimly. From his earliest years he had witnessed how fleeting love was for a Valtinos. A Valtinos *bought* love, paid well for its upkeep, got bored in exactly that order. His mother ran through young men as a lawnmower ran through grass. By the time Angel was in his twenties he was dealing with blackmail attempts, compromising photos and sordid scandals all on his mother's behalf. His mother had tremendous charm but she remained as immature and irresponsible as a teenager. Even so, she was the only mother he would ever have and at heart he was fond of her.

But he didn't get jealous or possessive of lovers because he didn't ever get attached to them or develop expectations of them. Expectations *always* led to disappointment. Merry, however, was in a different category because she was the mother of his daughter and Angel didn't want her to have another man in her life. That was a matter of simple good sense. Another man would divide her loyalties, take her focus off her child and invite unflattering comparisons...

'You heard the pitter patter of tiny feet and literally ran for the hills,' his brother Vitale had summed up a week earlier. 'Not a very promising beginning.'

No, it wasn't, Angel conceded wrathfully while endlessly scrutinising that photo in which his daughter appeared only as a small indistinct blob anchored in a pram. He had screwed up but he was a terrific strategist and unstoppable once he had a goal. He didn't even need an angle because his daughter was all the ammunition he required. Was Merry sleeping with that guy yet? Angel smouldered and scowled, beginning for the first time to scroll through the records he had studiously

ignored to respect Merry's privacy. To hell with
that scruple, he thought angrily. He had to fight
to protect what was *his*.

'So, how are you planning to play it with Elyssa's
father tomorrow?' Sybil asked that evening, having tried and failed to get much out of her niece
concerning the date with Fergus.

Merry shrugged. 'Cool, calm…'

'He's impossibly headstrong and obstinate,' her
aunt pronounced with disapproval. 'I only cocked
the gun because I didn't want him landing on your
doorstep unannounced but he wouldn't take no for
an answer.'

'He isn't familiar with the word no,' Merry
mused ruefully. 'I do wish I'd treated him to it
last year.'

'Do you really wish you didn't have Elyssa?'

Merry flushed and, thinking about that, shook
her head in dismissal. 'I thought I would when I
was pregnant but once she was here, everything
changed.'

'Maybe it changed for Angel as well. Maybe
he wasn't lying about that. He does value family
ties,' Sybil remarked.

Merry frowned. 'How do you know that?'

Sybil reddened, her eyes evasive. 'Well, you
told me he meets up with his father twice a month

and never cancels…and naturally I've read about his mother, Angelina's exploits in the newspapers. She's a real nut-job—rich, stupid, fickle. If he's still close to her, he has a high tolerance threshold for embarrassment. She's not far off my age and the men in her bed are getting younger by the year.'

Merry's eyes widened. 'I had no idea.'

'Shallow sexual relationships are all he saw growing up, all he's ever had as an example to follow. It's hardly surprising that he is the way he is. I won't excuse him for the way he treated you but I do see that he doesn't know any better,' Sybil completed, recognising Merry's surprise. 'But you could teach him different.'

'I don't think you can domesticate a wild animal.'

Sybil rolled her eyes. 'Elyssa has enough charisma to stop a charging rhinoceros.'

Merry tossed and turned in her bed, despising herself for her nervous tension. Angel had cast a long shadow over her afternoon with Fergus, depriving her of relaxation and appreciation. She had made hateful, unforgivable comparisons. On some secret, thoroughly inexcusable level, she still craved the buzz of excitement that Angel had filled her with and that unsettled and shamed her. After all, once the excitement had gone she had been left

pregnant and alone and now her memory trailed
back fifteen months...

Discovering that she was pregnant had proved a
real shock for Merry because she had not seriously
considered that that single accident was likely to
result in conception and had hoped for the best.
She had barely settled into a new and very challenging job, and falling pregnant had seemed like
the worst possible news. She had suffered from se-
vere morning sickness and at one stage had even
feared she was on the brink of having a miscarriage. She had waited until she was over three
months along before she'd even tried to contact
Angel to tell him that she was carrying his child.
She had never had his personal mobile number and
had never got to speak to him when she'd phoned
the office, suspecting that calls from her were on
some discreet forbidden list. The prospect of sending a letter or an email that would probably be
opened and read by a former colleague had made
her cringe. In the end she had used her working
knowledge of Angel's diary and had headed to
the hotel where he met his father for lunch twice
a month.

That unwise but desperate move had put in motion the most humiliating, wounding encounter of
Merry's life. Angel had had a very tall and beautiful blonde with him when he entered the bar, a

blonde with bare breasts on display under a gauzy
see-through dress. She had looked like the sort
of woman who didn't ever wear underwear and
every man in the place had stared lustfully at her,
while she'd clung to Angel's arm and giggled and
touched him with easy confidence. Just looking
at her, Merry had felt sick and ugly and plain and
boring because pregnancy had not been kind to
her. Her body had already been swelling and thick-
ening, her eyes had been shadowed because she
couldn't sleep and the smell of most foods had
made her nauseous. She had stayed concealed in
the bar behind a book and round a corner while
Angel, his companion and eventually his father
had sat down to lunch on an outside terrace.

If Angel had not reappeared at the bar alone,
she would probably simply have gone back to work
without even trying to achieve her goal. But when
she'd seen him she had forced herself up out of her
seat and forward.

'I have to speak to you in private,' she had said.
'It's very important. It will only take five minutes.'

He had spun back from the bar to appraise her
with cool, guarded eyes. 'I'm listening.'

'Could we go out into the foyer?' she had
pressed, very conscious of the number of people
around them. 'It would be more private.'

He had acquiesced with unconcealed reluctance. 'What is this about?' he had demanded as soon as they'd got there.

And then she had made her announcement and those expressive beautiful eyes of his had glittered like cold black diamonds, his consternation and annoyance obvious.

'Do you want it?' he had asked doubtingly, earning her hatred with every syllable of that leading question. 'Scratch that. It was politically incorrect. Of course, I will support you in whatever choice you make.' He had drawn out a business card and thrust it into her unwilling hand. 'I will inform my lawyers. Please provide them with contact details and I will make provision for you.'

And that had been Angel's knee-jerk response to unexpected fatherhood: brief and brutal and wholly unemotional and objective. *Go away and I'll give you cash to keep you quiet and at a distance.*

Remembering that encounter, Merry shuddered and tears stung her eyes afresh. That was the final moment when she had faced the reality that she had given her body to a ruthlessly detached man without a heart. How could she let such a man come within ten feet of her precious, loving daughter? That question kept her awake until dawn. Suddenly keeping the peace and giving Angel another chance seemed the stuff of stupidity.

* * *

Having done his baby research diligently before his visit, Angel believed he was prepared for all eventualities. His second cousin had six-month-old twins and a toddler and lived in London. It was hard to say who had been most startled by his interest: his cousin at the shock of his curiosity or Angel at finding himself festooned in wriggling babies, who cried, pooped and threw up while poking and pulling at him. There were loads of babies in his extended family circle but Angel had always given them a very wide berth.

He put on his oldest jeans for the occasion and, after consulting his cousin, he purchased only one modest gift. Merry wouldn't be impressed by a toyshop splurge. She was already saving every penny he was giving her into a trust for their daughter. Merry and her endless rainy-day fund, he thought incredulously, deeming her joyless, fearful attitude to spending money depressing. She was a natural-born hoarder of cash. If only his mother suffered from the same insecurity, he conceded wryly.

From upstairs, Merry watched the sleek, expensive car pull into the driveway. She had dressed smartly that morning. After all she had a potential new client coming at half eleven and she needed to look professional, so her hair was freshly washed, her make-up was on and she wore a summer dress that clung to her slender curves. What she wore had nothing whatsoever to do with Angel's visit, except in so far as looking smart lifted her confidence, she told herself soothingly.

Angel sprang fluidly out of his car, his lean, powerful body clad in black jeans and a green sweater that was undoubtedly cashmere. He found English summers cold. She carried Elyssa downstairs. Her daughter wore one of the fashionable baby outfits that Sybil often bought her, a pretty blue floral tunic and leggings that reflected her eyes. The door knocker rapped twice and she hastily settled Elyssa down on the rug before rushing breathlessly back to the door, scolding herself for the unmistakeable sense of anticipation gripping her.

Angel stepped in and his stunning dark golden gaze locked to her with the most electrifying immediacy. Tension leapt through Merry along with a growing unease about the decision she had made. He looked amazing. He *always* looked amazing, she reminded herself mockingly, striving not to react in any way. But it was impossible. Her breath shortened in her tightening throat and her breasts tingled and a sensual warmth made her thighs press together.

Angel's scrutiny roamed from the glossy bell

of her dark hair, down to the modest neckline of the dress that clung to the delectably full swell of her breasts, before skimming down over her waist to define the feminine swell of her hips. He didn't let himself look at her legs because she had fantastic legs and the heat pooling in his groin didn't need that added encouragement. He didn't know how she had contrived to get skinnier and at the same time more interestingly curvy but he especially didn't like the feeling of being sexually drawn against his will.

'Elyssa's in here,' she framed stiffly.

'That's a Greek name.'

'Yes, she's entitled to a Greek name,' Merry proclaimed defensively.

'I wasn't…criticising.' Angel registered the white-knuckled grip she had on the edge of the door and recognised that he would be treading on eggshells every time he spoke. He gritted his teeth on the awareness but as Merry pushed the door fully open he finally saw his daughter and for several timeless moments stayed rigid in the doorway drinking in the sight of her.

'She's got my hair,' he almost whispered, moving forward and then dropping down onto the rug a couple of feet from his daughter. 'But curls look cute on her…'

Merry watched him closely, registering that he

had enough sense not to try to get too familiar too fast with a baby that didn't know him. No, Angel was far too clever to make an obvious wrong move, she reflected bitterly, before catching herself up on that suspicious but hardly charitable thought and crossing the room to go into the kitchen. 'Coffee?'

'If it's not too much trouble.'

'Don't go all polite on me,' she said drily.

'What do you expect?' Angel shot her a sardonic glance of rebuke. 'I know you don't want me here.'

Merry paled at that blunt statement. 'I'm trying not to feel like that.'

She put on the kettle and watched him remove a toy from his pocket, a brightly coloured teething toy, which he set on the rug at his feet. It was a strategic move and Elyssa quickly fulfilled his expectations by extending the toy she held to him in the hope of gaining access to the new and more interesting one. Angel accepted it and handed over his gift. Elyssa chortled with satisfaction and bestowed a huge smile on him before sticking the new toy into her mouth and chewing happily on it.

'She has your eyes,' Angel remarked. 'She's incredibly pretty.'

In spite of her desire to remain unmoved, Merry flushed with pride. 'I think so too.'

'She's also unmistakeably mine,' Angel intoned with unashamed approval.

'Well, you already knew that,' Merry could not resist reminding him. 'She was DNA tested after she was born.'

Angel winced. 'I never once doubted that the child you were carrying was mine but in view of inheritance rights…and us not being married…it was best to have it legally confirmed.' He hesitated before turning his classic bronzed profile to study her levelly. 'But I let the lawyers take over and run the whole show and that was a mistake. I see that now.'

Merry jerked her chin in acknowledgement, not trusting herself to speak.

'I didn't know any other way to handle it,' Angel admitted grimly. 'I took the easy way out… unfortunately the easy way turned out to be the wrong way.'

Taken aback by that admission, Merry dragged in a ragged breath and turned away to make the coffee. A fat burst of chuckles from her daughter made her flip back and she saw Elyssa bouncing on the rug, held steady by Angel's hands and revelling in both the exercise and the attention.

When Elyssa tired of that, Angel turned out her toy box for her. Tiger slunk out from under the chair where he had been hiding since Angel's arrival and moved hesitantly closer to investigate.

'Diavolos!' Angel exclaimed in surprise. 'Where did the dog come from?'

Startled by Angel's deep voice, Tiger shot back under the chair.

'He's been here all along. His name's Tiger.'

'Kind of nervous for a dog called Tiger and hardly a stream-lined predator.'

'OK. He's fat, you can say it. He's addicted to food and he wasn't socialised properly when he was young. He came from a puppy farm that was closed down,' Merry volunteered, extending a cup of black coffee to Angel as he vaulted lithely upright, suddenly dominating the small room with his height and the breadth of his shoulders.

'I didn't know you were keen on dogs.'

'I practically grew up helping in the rescue centre.' Merry could hear herself gabbling because her heart was pounding wildly in her chest as Angel moved towards her and even breathing was a challenge beneath the onslaught of his gleaming dark golden eyes. 'I—'

'Tell it like it is,' Angel urged sibilantly.

Her smooth brow furrowed. 'What are you talking about?'

'You still want me as much as I want you,' he breathed huskily, sipping his coffee as if he were merely making casual conversation.

'I don't want to have that sort of discussion with

you,' Merry told him curtly, colour burnishing her cheeks as she wondered if he really could tell that easily that she was still vulnerable around him. Not that she would do anything about it or let *him* do anything about it, she reasoned with pride. Attraction was nothing more than a hormonal trick and, in her case, a very dangerous misdirection.

'Avoid? Deny?' Angel derided, his beautiful wilful mouth curling, his smouldering gaze enhanced by unfairly long black lashes welded to her fast-reddening face. 'What's the point?'

'If you continue this I'm going to ask you to leave,' Merry warned thinly.

And genuine amusement engulfed Angel and laughter lit up his lean, dark features. 'I'm not about to pounce on you with our daughter watching! Believe me, while she's around, you're safe,' he assured her smoothly.

Inexplicably that little exchange made Merry feel foolish and rather as though she had ended up with egg on her face, which was burning like a furnace. Even now, many months after the event, she couldn't laugh about what had happened between them. Looking back, it was as if blinding sunlight overlaid and blurred the explosive passion she couldn't begin to explain and never wanted to experience again. Unfortunately for her, her body had a different ambition. One glimpse of Angel's darkly handsome face and long, sleek, muscular frame and she was as tense as a bowstring, caught between forbidden pleasure at his sheer physical beauty and angry self-loathing at her susceptibility to it.

'I brought lunch with me,' Angel revealed, startling her.

Her eyes widened. 'But I have a client due.'

'I'll return in an hour. You know we need to talk about Elyssa and how we move on from here,' Angel pointed out as if it were the most reasonable and natural thing in the world when in truth they had never ever talked about anything.

'Yes…yes, of course,' she muttered uneasily, because she could see that a talk made sense and it was surely better to get it all over in one go and in one day, she told herself soothingly. 'I should be free in an hour, but—'

'I'll make it an hour and a half,' Angel cut in decisively as he moved towards the door.

Merry skimmed his arm with an uncertain finger to attract his attention. 'I'm afraid Elyssa has…er…stained your sweater,' she told him awkwardly.

His amused grin flashed perfect white teeth and enhanced the sculpted fullness of his wide, sensual mouth. 'It's not a problem. I brought a change of clothes with me.'

'My goodness, you were organised,' she mumbled in surprise as he strode down the path and leant down into his car, straightening to peel off the offending sweater and expose the flexing muscles of his bronzed and powerful torso. Her mouth ran dry and she stared, watching him pull on another sweater, black this time, before she closed the door.

She ignored her reeling senses to concentrate on what was truly important. Angel was unpredictable, she reminded herself worriedly, devious to a fault and dangerously volatile. What did he truly want from her? Why was he putting himself to so much trouble? *Lunch?* All of a sudden he was bringing her lunch? Merry was stunned by the concept and the planning that must have gone into that. Did Angel really want access to his daughter *that* badly? Did he have sufficient interest and staying power to want a long-term relationship with his daughter? And where did that leave her when she really didn't want Angel to feature *anywhere* in her life?

You should've thought of that before you let him visit, Merry told herself in exasperation. Possibly Angel was only trying to smooth over the hostilities between them. And possibly she was a suspicious little shrew, still bitter and battered from her previous encounters with him. At the very least she ought to acknowledge that she would never ever second-guess Angel Valtinos and that he would always take her by surprise. After all, that was how he did business and how he thrived in a cut-throat world.

CHAPTER FIVE

MERRY SHOOK HANDS with her new client, who had got into a mess with his tax returns, and promised to update him on the situation within the week. Soon she would have to try to fit in a refresher course to update her knowledge of recent legislative changes, she reflected thoughtfully, incredibly keen to think of anything other than the awareness that Angel was sliding supple as a dancer out of his car as her visitor departed.

Sybil had swooped in to take enthusiastic charge of Elyssa soon after Angel's earlier departure. Hearing of the lunch plan, she had laughed and drily observed, 'He's treating you to a charm offensive. Well, if you must have a serious talk with him, it'll be easier not to have Elyssa grizzling for her lunch and her nap in the midst of it. Phone me when you want to steal her back.'

And once again, Merry had reflected how very,

very lucky she had always been to have Sybil in her life, standing by her when life was tough, advising and supporting her, in short being the only caring mother figure that she had ever known. Sybil had cured the hurts inflicted by her kid sister's lack of interest in and impatience with her child and, although Merry knew her aunt had been disappointed when she became pregnant without being in a serious relationship, she had kept her disappointment to herself and had instead focused her attention on how best to help her expectant niece.

'Lunch,' Angel told her carelessly, carting a large luxurious hamper in one hand.

'I've got a terrace out the back. Since it's sunny, we might as well eat there,' Merry suggested, preferring the idea of that casual setting in which she thought Angel would be less intimidating.

'This is unexpectedly pleasant,' Angel remarked, sprawling down with innate grace on a wrought-iron chair and taking in the pleasant view of fields and wooded hills visible beyond the hedge.

'This was Sybil's Christmas surprise for us,' Merry explained. 'Her last tenant was elderly and the garden was overgrown. Sybil hired someone to fix it up and now Elyssa will have somewhere safe to play when she's more mobile.'

'You're very close to your aunt,' Angel commented warily. 'She doesn't like me.'

Crystalline blue eyes collided with his in challenge. 'What did you expect?' she traded.

Angel had not been prepared to meet with a condemnation that bold and unapologetic and his teeth clenched, squaring his aggressive jaw, the faint dark shadow of stubble already roughening his bronzed skin accentuating the hard slant of his shapely mouth.

'Yes, you ensured I had enough money to survive but that was that,' Merry stated before he could remind her of the reality.

Angel sidestepped that deeply controversial issue by ignoring it. Instead he opened the hamper and stacked utensils and dishes on the table and asked where his daughter was. After all, what could he say about his treatment of Merry? The facts were the facts and he couldn't change them. He knew he had done everything wrong and he had acknowledged that. Didn't his honesty and his regret lighten the scales even a little? Was she expecting him to grovel on hands and knees?

'Wow…this is some spread,' Merry remarked uneasily as she set out the food and he uncorked the bottle of wine and filled the glasses with rich red liquid. 'Where did it come from?'

'From one of my hotels,' Angel responded with

the nonchalance that was the sole preserve of the very rich.

Merry placed a modest selection of savoury bites on her plate and said tensely, 'What did you want to discuss?'

'Our future,' Angel delivered succinctly while Tiger sat at his feet with little round pleading eyes pinned to the meat on his fork.

'Nobody can foretell the future,' Merry objected.

'I can where we're concerned,' Angel assured her, every liquid syllable cool as ice. 'Either we spend at least the next ten years fighting it out over Elyssa in court or...we get married and *share* her.'

Merry studied him over the top of her wine glass with steadily widening pale blue eyes, and then gulped in more wine than she intended and coughed and spluttered in the most embarrassing manner as she struggled to get a grip on her wildly fluctuating emotions. First he had frightened the life out of her by mentioning a court battle over her beloved daughter, and then he'd sent her spinning with a suggestion she had never dreamt that she would hear from his lips.

'*Married?*' she emphasised with a curled lip. 'Are you crazy or just trying to unnerve me?'

Having forced himself to pull the pin on the marriage grenade straight away, Angel coiled back in his chair and savoured his wine. 'It's an unnerving idea for me as well. Apart from my mother, who wanders in and out of my properties, I've never lived with a woman before,' he admitted curtly. 'But we do need to think creatively to solve our current problems.'

'I don't have any problems right now. I also can't believe that you want Elyssa so much after one little meeting that you would sink to what is virtually blackmail,' Merry framed coldly, eyes glinting like chipped ice in the sunlight.

'Oh, I would sink a lot lower than that and I think you know it,' Angel traded without shame, unyielding dark golden eyes steady with stubborn resolve. 'I will do whatever I have to do to get what I want…or in this case to ensure that my daughter benefits from a suitable home.'

'But Elyssa already *has* a suitable home,' Merry pointed out, working hard to stay calm and appear untouched by his threat of legal intervention. 'We're happy here. I have work that I can do at home and we have a decent life.'

'Only not by my standards. Elyssa is my heir and will one day be a very wealthy woman. When you're so prejudiced against spending my money, how do you expect her to adapt to my world when she becomes independent?' he demanded with lethal cool.

Merry compressed her sultry mouth and lifted angrily out of her seat. 'I'm not prejudiced!' she protested. 'I didn't want to *depend* on your money. I simply prefer to stand on my own feet.'

Angel dealt her a perceptive appraisal that made her skin tighten uneasily over her bones. 'Like me, you have trust issues and you're very proud.'

'Don't you tell me that I have trust issues when you know absolutely nothing about me!' Merry practically spat back at him in her fury. 'Newsflash, Angel…we had two sexual encounters, *not* a relationship!'

Angel ran lingering hooded dark eyes over her slender figure and her aggressive stance, remembering that fire in bed, how it had stoked his own and resulted in a conflagration more passionate than anything he had ever known. As a rule, she kept that fire hidden, suppressed beneath her tranquil, prissy little surface, but around him she couldn't manage that feat and he cherished that truth. Anger was much more promising than indifference.

Merry planted her hands on her curvy hips and flung him a fierce look of censure. 'And don't you *dare* look at me like that!' she warned him, helplessly conscious of that smouldering sexual assessment. 'It's rude and inappropriate.'

Angel shifted lithely in his chair, murderously aware of his roaring arousal and the tightness of his jeans and marvelling at the reality that he could actually be enjoying himself in her company, difficult though she was. A slow-burning smile slashed his lean, strong face. 'The burn is still there, *glyka mou*,' he told her. 'But let's concentrate our energies on my solution for our future.'

'That wasn't a solution, that was fanciful nonsense!' Merry hissed back at him. 'You don't want to marry me. You don't want to marry anybody!'

'But I'll do it for Elyssa's benefit because I believe that she needs a father as much as she needs a mother,' Angel asserted levelly. 'A father is not expendable. My father was very important in my life, even though he wasn't able to be there for me as much as he would have liked.'

Unprepared for that level of honesty and gravity from a man as naturally secretive and aloof as Angel, Merry was bemused. 'I never said you were expendable, for goodness' sake,' she argued less angrily. 'That's why I let you finally visit and meet her.'

'How much of a relationship did you have with your own father?' Angel enquired lethally.

Merry's face froze. 'I didn't have one. My mother, Natalie, fell pregnant by her boss and he was married. I met him once but his wife couldn't stand the sight of me, probably because I was the proof of his infidelity,' she conceded uncomfortably. 'He never asked to see me again. When it came to making a choice between me and his wife, naturally he chose his wife.'

'I'm sorry.' Angel disconcerted her with a look of sympathy that hurt her pride as much as a slap would have done.

'Well, I'm not. I got by fine without him,' Merry declared, lifting her chin.

'Maybe you did.' Angel trailed out the word, letting her know he wasn't convinced by her face-saving claim. 'But others don't do so well without paternal guidance. My own mother grew up indulged in every financial way, but essentially without parents who cared enough about her to discipline her. She's well past fifty now, although she doesn't look it, but she's still a rebellious teenager in her own head. I want my daughter to have stability. I don't want her to go wild when she becomes an adult with the world at her feet along with every temptation.'

Involuntarily impressed by that argument, Merry shook her head. 'That's a long way off and if I don't stand in the way of her having a relationship with you now, you'll still be around.'

Angel lounged back in his chair and crossed an ankle over one knee, long, powerful thigh muscles flexing below tight, faded denim. He looked outrageously relaxed, as if he were posing for a publicity shot, and drop-dead gorgeous from the spill of glossy black curls to the golden caramel brilliance of his eyes. Merry dragged her guilty gaze from his thighs and his crotch, sudden heat rising inside her and burning her cheeks. His hard-boned, thoroughly raunchy masculine beauty broke through her defences every time she looked at him and it made her feel like a breathless fan girl.

'But the bottom line is that unless we marry I won't be around *enough*,' Angel intoned with grim emphasis. 'I spend at least fifty per cent of the year abroad. I want her to meet my relatives and learn what it means to be a Valtinos…'

He could have said nothing more calculated to cool Merry's fevered response to him. Dismay filled her because she understood the message he was giving her. As soon as Elyssa was old enough, Angel would be spiriting her out to Greece, taking her away from her mother, leaving Merry behind, shorn of control of what happened in her child's life. It was a sobering prospect.

'Did you mean it…what you said about fighting me in court?' Merry prompted angrily.

'For once in my life I was playing it straight,' Angel declared.

'But where the heck did all this suddenly come

from?' Merry demanded in heated denial. 'You didn't want anything to do with us last winter!'

'It took time for me to come to terms with how I felt about fatherhood. At first I thought the most important objective was to conserve my world as it was. I thought I could turn my back on you and my child but I found that I couldn't,' Angel breathed in a roughened undertone as though the words were being extracted forcibly from him. 'I couldn't stop thinking about her…or you.'

'Me?' Merry gasped in sharp disbelief. 'Why would you have been thinking about me?'

Angel lifted and dropped a broad shoulder in questioning doubt. 'So, I'm human. Learning that a woman is carrying your child is an unexpectedly powerful discovery—'

'Angel,' Merry cut in without hesitation, 'let's come back down to earth here. Learning that I was pregnant sent you into retreat so fast you left a smoke trail in your wake!'

'And all I learned was that there was no place to run from reality,' Angel countered with sardonic bite. 'I fought my curiosity for a long time before I finally gave way to it and asked to see her. You said no repeatedly but here we are now, supposedly acting like adults. I'm *trying* to be honest… I'm *trying* not to threaten you but I've come to see marriage as the best option for all three of us.'

'You threatened me quite deliberately!' Merry slung at him furiously.

'You need to know that I'm serious and that this is not some whim that will go away if you wait for long enough. I'm here to stay in your lives,' Angel intoned harshly.

'Well, that's going to be rather awkward when it's not what I want and I will fight you every step of the way!' Merry flung back at him. 'You wanted me out of your life and I got out. You can't force me back.'

'If it means my daughter gets the future she deserves, I will force you,' Angel bit out in a raw, wrathful undertone as he plunged upright, casting a long dark shadow over the table. 'You need to accept that this is not just about you and me any more, it's about *her*!'

Merry paled. 'I do accept that.'

'No, you don't. You're still set on punishing me for the selfish decisions I made and that approach isn't going to get us anywhere. I don't *want* to go to court and fight but I *will* if I have no alternative!' Angel shot at her furiously, dark golden eyes scorching, his Greek accent edging every vowel with piercing sibilance in the afternoon stillness. 'When I asked you to marry me I was trying to show respect!'

'You wouldn't know respect if it bit you on the

arse!' Merry flamed back at him with helpless vul-
garity. 'And I am so sorry I didn't grovel with grat-
itude at the offer of a wedding ring the way you
obviously expected.'

'No, you're not sorry!' Angel roared back at her
equally loudly. 'You enjoyed dragging me over
the coals, questioning my motivation and commitment, and not for one minute did you seriously
consider what I was offering…'

'Stop shouting at me!' Merry warned him, reeling in shock from that sudden volatile surge of
anger from him, not having appreciated that that
rage could lie so close to his seemingly cool surface.

'I've said sorry every damn way I know how
but you're after revenge, not a way forward, and
there's nothing I can do to change that!' Angel
growled, throwing open the back door to go back
into the house and leave.

There was sufficient truth in that stormy welter
of accusations to draw Merry up short and make
her question her attitude. 'I'm not after revenge…
that's ridiculous!' she protested weakly, closing a
staying hand over his arm as he shot her yet another murderous smouldering glance before turning back to the door.

Sorry every damn way I know how rang afresh

in her ears and tightened her grip on his muscular forearm. 'Angel, please…let's calm down.'

'For what good reason would I calm down?' Angel raked down at her. 'This was a pointless attempt on my part to change things between us.'

Her teeth were chattering with nerves. 'Yes, I can see that but you storming off in a rage is only going to make things worse,' she muttered ruefully. 'Maybe I haven't been fair to you, maybe I haven't given you a decent hearing, but you came at me with this like a rocket out of nowhere and I don't adapt quickly to new ideas the way you do!'

'You adapted fast enough to me in bed!' Angel husked with sizzling clarity.

'That's your massive ego talking!' Merry launched back at him irately.

'No, it's not,' Angel growled, yanking her up against him, shifting his lithe hips, ensuring she recognised how turned-on he was. 'You make me want you.'

'It's *my* fault?' Merry carolled in disbelief even as her whole body tilted into his, as magnetised by his arousal as a thirsty plant suddenly placed within reach of water. Little tremors were running through her as she struggled to get a grip on the prickling tightness of her nipples and the heat building between her thighs. An unbearable ache followed that she positively shrank from re-living in his vicinity. She wanted to slap herself, she wanted to slap him, she wanted to freeze the moment and replay it *her* way, in which she would draw back from him in withering disgust and say something terribly clever and wounding that would hold him at bay.

'You just can't bring yourself to admit that you're the same,' Angel gritted, bending his arrogant dark head, one hand meshing into the tumble of her hair to drag her head back and expose her throat. His mouth found that slender corded column and nipped and tasted up to her ear, awakening a shower of tingling sensation, and she was electrified and dizzy with longing, wanting what she knew she shouldn't, wanting with a hunger suppressed and denied for too many months, craving the release he could give.

And then he kissed her, crushing her ripe mouth, his tongue plunging and retreating, and she saw stars and whirling multicoloured planets behind her lowered lids while her body fizzed like a firework display, leaving her weak with hunger. She kissed him back, hands rising to delve into the crisp luxuriance of his hair, framing, holding, *needing*. It was frantic, out of control, the way it always was for them.

Angel wrenched her back from him, long brown fingers biting into her slim shoulders to keep her upright and gazing up into his blazing liquid-honey eyes. 'No, I'm not a one-trick pony or a cheap one-night stand. You'll have to marry me to get any more of that,' he told her with derision as he slapped a business card down on the table. 'My phone number…should you think better of your attitude today.'

When he was gone, Merry paced back and forth in her small sitting room, facing certain realities. She hadn't seriously considered Angel's supposed solution. But then that was more his fault than her own. Warning her that he intended to trail her into court and fight for access to their daughter had scarcely acted as a good introduction to his alternative offer. She was angry and bitter and she wasn't about to apologise for the fact, but possibly she should have listened and asked more and lost her temper less.

In addition, Angel's visit had worsened rather than improved their relations because now she knew he was prepared to drag her through the courts in an effort to win greater access to Elyssa. And what if his ambitions did not stop there? What if he intended to try and gain sole custody of their daughter and take Elyssa away from her? Paling and breathing rapidly, Merry decided to visit her aunt and discuss her mounting concern and sense of being under threat with her.

Sybil, however, was nowhere to be found in the comfortable open-plan ground floor of her home and it was only when Merry heard her daughter that she realised her aunt and her daughter were upstairs. She was disconcerted to walk into Sybil's bedroom where Elyssa was playing on the floor and find her aunt trailing clothes out of the wardrobes to pile into the two suitcases sitting open on the bed.

'My goodness, where are you going?' Merry demanded in surprise.

Sybil dealt her a shamefaced glance. 'I meant to phone you but I had so many other calls to make that I didn't get a chance. Your mother's in trouble and I'm flying out to Perth to be with her,' she told her.

Merry blinked in astonishment. 'Trouble?' she queried.

Sybil grimaced. 'Keith's been having an affair and he's walked out on your mother. She's suicidal, poor lamb.'

'Oh, dear,' Merry framed, sinking down on the edge of the bed to lift her daughter onto her lap. She was sad to hear that news, but her troubled relationship with her dysfunctional parent prevented her from feeling truly sympathetic and that fact always filled her with remorse. Not for the first time she marvelled that Sybil could be so forgiving of her kid sister's frailties. Time and time again she had watched her aunt wade into Natalie's emotional dramas and rush to sort them out with infinite supportive compassion. Sometimes, too, Merry wondered why it was that she, Natalie's daughter, could not be so forgiving, so tolerant, so willing to offer another fresh chance. Possibly that could be because Merry remembered Natalie's resentment of her as a child too strongly, she told herself guiltily. Natalie hadn't wanted to be anyone's Mummy and her constant rejections had deeply wounded Merry.

'Oh, dear, indeed,' her aunt sighed worriedly. 'Natalie was distraught when she phoned me and you *know* she does stupid things when she's upset! She really shouldn't be alone right now.'

'Doesn't she have any friends out there?' Merry prompted.

Sybil frowned, clearly finding Merry's response unfeeling. 'Family's family and you and her don't get on well enough for you to go. Nor would it be right to subject Elyssa to that journey. Natalie wouldn't want a baby around either,' she conceded ruefully.

'She really can't be bothered with young children,' Merry agreed wryly. 'Do you *have* to go?'

Sybil looked pained by that question. 'Merry, she's got nobody else!' she proclaimed, sharply defensive in both speech and manner. 'Of course, that means I'm landing you with looking after things here…will you be able to manage the centre? Nicky is free to take over for you from next week. I've already spoken to her about it. Between minding Elyssa and running your own business, you're not able to drop everything for me right now.'

'But I would've managed,' Merry assured the older woman, resisting the urge to protest her aunt's decision to call on the help of an old friend, rather than her niece. Seeing the lines of tension and anxiety already indenting Sybil's face, Merry decided to keep what had happened with Angel to herself. Right now, her aunt had enough on her plate and didn't need any additional stress from Merry's corner.

That evening, once Elyssa was bathed and tucked into her cot, Merry opened a bottle of wine. Sybil had already departed for the first flight she had been able to book and Merry was feeling more than a little lonely. She lifted her laptop and put Angel's name into a search engine. It was something she had never allowed herself to do before, deeming any such information-gathering online to be unhealthy and potentially obsessional. Now drinking her wine, she didn't care any more because her spirits were low and in need of distraction.

A cascade of photos lined up and in a driven mood of defiance she clicked on them one after another. Unsurprisingly, Angel looked shockingly good in pictures. Her lip curled and she refilled her glass, sipping it while she browsed, only to freeze when she saw the most recent photo of Angel with the same blonde he had brought to lunch with his father the day Merry had told him that she was pregnant. That photo had been taken only the night before at some charitable benefit: Angel, the ultimate in the socialite stakes in a designer dinner jacket, smooth and sleek and gorgeous, and his blonde companion, Roula Paulides, ravishing in a tight glittering dress that exposed an astonishing amount of her chest.

She was Greek too, a woman Angel would presumably have much more in common with. Merry fiercely battled the urge to do an online search on Roula as well. What was she? A stalker?

She finished her glass of wine and grabbed the bottle up in a defiant move to fill the glass again. Well, she was glad she had looked, wasn't she?

"*4 for 4*" MINI-SURVEY

We are prepared to **REWARD** you with 2 FREE books and 2 FREE gifts for completing our MINI SURVEY!

FREE Value Over $20!

You'll get...

TWO FREE BOOKS & TWO FREE GIFTS

just for participating in our Mini Survey!

Dear Reader,

IT'S A FACT: if you answer 4 quick questions, we'll send you **4 FREE REWARDS!**

I'm not kidding you. As a leading publisher of women's fiction, we value your opinions... and your time. That's why we are prepared to **reward** you handsomely for completing our mini-survey. In fact, we have 4 Free Rewards for you, including 2 free books and 2 free gifts.

As you may have guessed, that's why our mini-survey is called **"4 for 4".** Answer 4 questions and get 4 Free Rewards. It's that simple!

Thank you for participating in our survey,

Pam Powers

The very night before he proposed marriage to Merry, Angel had been in another woman's company and had probably spent the night in her bed. Even worse the sexy blonde was clearly an unusual woman, being one who was an enduring interest in Angel's life and not one of the more normal options, who swanned briefly on scene and then was never seen again with him.

Merry fought the turbulent swell of emotion tightening her chest, denying that it hurt, denying that it bothered her in the slightest to discover that Angel was still seeing that same blonde all these many months later. But denial didn't work in the mood she was in as she sat sipping her wine and staring into the middle distance, angry bitterness threatening to consume her.

How *dared* he propose to her only hours after being in another woman's company? How *dared* he condemn her for not taking him seriously? And how dared he come on to her as he had out on the terrace before he'd left? Didn't he have any morals at all? Any conscience? And how could she even begin to be jealous over such a brazen, incurable playboy?

And yet she *was* jealous, Merry acknowledged wretchedly, stupidly, pointlessly jealous of a thoroughly fickle, unreliable man. Rage flared inside

her afresh as she recalled that careless suggestion
that they marry. Oh, he had played that marriage
proposal down, all right, shoving it on the table
without ceremony or even a hint of romance. Was
it any wonder that she had not taken that suggestion seriously?

In a sudden movement Merry flew out of her
seat and stalked out to the kitchen to lift the business card Angel had left with her. She was texting
him before she had even thought through what she
wanted to say…

Do you realise that if you married me you would
have to give up other women?

Angel studied the screen of his phone in disbelief. He was dining with his brother Vitale and the
sudden text from an unfamiliar number that be-
longed to Merry took him aback. He breathed in
deep, his wide, sensual mouth compressing with
exasperation.

Are you finally taking me seriously? If I married
you there would be NO OTHER WOMEN.

Merry had texted him in shouty capitals.
'Problems?' Vitale hazarded.
Angel shook his dark head and grinned while

wondering if Merry was drunk. He just could not imagine her being that blunt otherwise. Merry of all women drunk-dialling him, Merry who was always so careful, so restrained. A sudden and quite shocking degree of wondering satisfaction gripped Angel, washing away his edgy tension, his conviction that he had made a fatal misstep with her and a hash of their meeting.

And no other men for you either.

He pointed this out with pleasure in his reply.

That wasn't a problem for Merry, who was stunned that he was replying to her so quickly. In truth, she had never ever wanted anyone as much as she wanted Angel Valtinos. All thoughts of kindly and dependable Fergus flew from her mind. She didn't like the fact and certainly wasn't proud of it. Indeed, she wouldn't have admitted it even if Angel slow-roasted her over an open fire but it was, indisputably, the secret reality she lived with.

'Who are you texting?' his brother demanded.

'My daughter's mother.' Angel shot his sibling a triumphant glance. 'I believe that you will be standing up at my wedding for me as soon as I can get it arranged.'

Vitale frowned. 'I thought you crashed and burned?'

'Obviously not,' Angel savoured, still texting, keener yet to get a clear response.

Exclusivity approved. Are you agreeing to marry me?

Merry froze, suddenly shocked back to real life and questioning what she was doing. What *was* she doing? Raging, burning jealousy had almost eaten her alive when she saw that blonde with him again.

We'd have to talk about that.

I'm a doer, not a talker. You have to give me a chance.

But he'd had his chance with her and wrecked it, Merry reminded herself feverishly. He didn't do feelings or proper relationships outside his own family circle. Yet there was something curiously and temptingly seductive about proud, arrogant Angel asking *her* to give *him* another chance.

She decided to give him a warning.

One LAST chance.

* * *

YES! WE HAVE A DEAL!

Angel texted back with amusement and an intense sense of achievement.

He had won. He had gained his daughter, the precious chance to bring Elyssa into his life instead of losing her. In addition, he would be gaining a wife, a very unusual wife, who didn't want his money. Another man would have celebrated that reality but, when it came to women, Angel was always suspicious, always looking out for hidden motives and secret objectives. Women were complicated, which was why he never got involved and never dipped below the shallow surface with his lovers…and Merry was infinitely *more* complicated than the kind of women he was familiar with.

Could such a marriage work?

Only time would tell, he reflected with uncharacteristic gravity. No other women, he pondered abstractedly. Well, he hadn't been prepared for that demand, he acknowledged ruefully, having proposed marriage while intending the union as more of a convenient parental partnership than anything more personal. After all, he knew several couples who contrived to lead separate lives below the same roof while remaining safely married. They stayed together for the sake of their children or to protect their wealth from the damage of divorce, but nothing more emotional was involved.

In reality, Angel had never seen anything positive about the marital state. The official Valtinos outlook on marriage was that it was generally disastrous and extremely expensive. His own mother's infidelity had ensured that his parents had parted by the time he was four years old. His grandparents had enjoyed an equally calamitous union while shunning divorce in favour of living in separate wings of the same house. Nor was Angel's attitude softened by the number of cheating spouses he had met over the years. In his early twenties, Angel had automatically assumed that he would never marry.

But, self-evidently, Merry had a very different take on marriage and parenthood, a much more conventional take than a cynical and distrustful Valtinos. Here she was demanding fidelity upfront as though it was the very bedrock of stability. And maybe it *was*, Angel conceded dimly, reflecting on the constant turmoil caused by his mother's rampant promiscuity. He thought equally hard about the little scene of apparent domestic contentment he had glimpsed at his cousin's house, where a husband rushed into his home to greet a wife and children whom he obviously valued and missed. That glimpse had provided Angel with a disturbing vision of another world that had never been visible to him before, a much more personalised and intimate version of marriage.

And Merry, it seemed, had chosen to view his suggestion of marriage as being personal, *very* personal, rather than practical as he had envisioned. Beneath his brother's exasperated gaze, Angel lounged back in his dining chair, his meal untouched, and for the first time in his life smiled with slashing brilliance at the prospect of acquiring a wife and a wedding ring...

CHAPTER SIX

'You SHOULD'VE WARNED Angelina,' Charles Russell censured his son while they waited at the church. 'Your mother isn't ready to be a grandmother.'

'Tough,' Angel dismissed with sardonic bite. 'I'm thirty-three, not a teenager. It shouldn't be that much of a surprise.'

Always more sympathetic to other people's vulnerabilities, Charles sighed. 'She can't help being vain. She is what she is. By not telling her in advance, you're risking her causing a scene.'

On her way to the church that same morning, Merry was lost in the weird daze that had engulfed her from the moment she had agreed by text to marry Angel. She was stunned by what she had done in the hold of more wine and jealousy than sense but, in the two weeks that had passed, any urge to renege on the deal Angel had named it had slowly faded away. She wasn't willing to walk away from Angel Valtinos and face a court battle for custody of her daughter. She was also fully aware that he had blackmailed her into marriage and was quite unsurprised by his ruthlessness, having seen how he operated on the business front.

Angel would undoubtedly hurt her but when push came to shove she had decided that she would infinitely rather have him as a husband than not have him at all. He would be hers with a ring on his finger and she would have to settle for that level of commitment, was certainly not building any little fantasies in which Angel, the unfeeling, would start doing feelings. She was trying to be realistic, trying to be practical about their prospects and she would have been happier on her wedding day had she not somehow contrived to have a massively upsetting row with Sybil about her plans.

Quite how that dreadful schism had opened, Merry had no very clear idea. Her aunt had been understandably shocked and astonished when Merry had phoned her in Australia to announce that she was getting married. Sybil had urged her to wait until she got home and could discuss that major step with her. But Merry, fearful of losing her nerve to marry a man who did not love her, had refused to wait and Sybil had taken that refusal to wait for her counsel badly. The more Sybil had criticised Angel and his reputation as a womaniser, the stiffer and more stubborn Merry had become.

She was very well acquainted with Angel's flaws but had not enjoyed having them rammed down her throat in very blunt words by her protective aunt. It was all very well, she had realised, for *her* to criticise Angel, but inexplicably something else entirely for anyone else to do it.

And throughout the past tumultuous and busy two weeks, Angel had been terrific in trying to organise everything to ensure that Merry could cope with the gigantic life change he was inflicting on her. Unfortunately, it was also true that between their various commitments they had barely seen each other. Handing Tiger over to the new owner Sybil had approved had been upsetting because she had become very fond of the little dog and only hoped that his quirks would not irritate in his new home.

Angel had had so much business to take care of while Merry had been engaged in closing down her own business and packing. Even so, Angel had managed to meet with her twice in London to see Elyssa and in his unfamiliar restraint she had recognised the same desire not to rock the boat that beat like an unnerving storm warning through her every fibre. He had been very detached but playful and surprisingly hands-on with Elyssa. It was clear to her that Angel didn't want to risk doing anything that could potentially disrupt their marital plans and deprive him of shared custody of their daughter.

Of course it would take time for Angel to adapt to the idea of marriage and a family of his own and Merry appreciated that reality. He wasn't going to be perfect from the word go, but the imperfect that warned her that he was trying hard was enough to satisfy her…admittedly somewhat low…expectations. She couldn't set the bar too high for him at the start, she told herself urgently. She had to compromise and concentrate on what was truly important.

And what could be more important than Elyssa and seizing the opportunity to provide her daughter with a father? Merry knew what it was like to live with a yawning space in her paternal background. She had never known her father and, unpleasant though it was to acknowledge, her father hadn't cared enough to seek her out to get to know her. But Angel *was* making that effort, right down to having interviewed nannies with Merry to find the one he thought would be most suitable. Entirely raised by nannies before boarding school, Angel had contrived to ask questions that wouldn't even have occurred to Merry and she had been impressed by his concern on their daughter's behalf and his determination to choose the most caring candidate.

So what if his input on the actual wedding and their future relationship had been virtually non-existent? He had hired a wedding organiser to take care of the arrangements and hadn't seemed to care in the slightest about the details that had unexpectedly consumed Merry. Was that just Angel being a man or a dangerous sign that he couldn't care less about the woman he was about to marry? Merry stifled a shiver, rammed down the fear that had flared and contemplated her manicured fingernails with rampant nervous tension. She had made her choice and she had to live with it when the alternative was so much worse and so much emptier. Surely it was better to give marriage a chance?

It had been embarrassing to tell Fergus that she was marrying Angel but he had taken the news in good part, possibly having already worked out that she was still far from indifferent to her daughter's father.

The first shock of Merry's wedding day was the unexpected sight of Sybil waiting on the church steps, a tall, slender figure attired in a very elegant blue dress and brimmed hat. Eyes wide with astonishment, Merry emerged from the limousine that had ferried her to the church from the hotel where she had stayed the night before and exclaimed in shaken disbelief, '*Sybil?*'

'Obviously I couldn't miss your big day, darling.

I got back in the early hours,' Sybil breathed with a revealing shimmer in her eyes as she reached for Merry's hand. 'I'm so sorry about the things I said. I overstepped, *interfered*—'

'No, I was too touchy!' Merry slotted in, stretching up on tiptoe to press a forgiving kiss to the older woman's cheek. 'You were shocked, of course you were.'

'Yes, especially as you're contriving to do what I never managed…you're getting married,' Sybil murmured fondly. 'And you didn't do too badly at all picking that dress without my advice. It's a stunner.'

Her heartache subsiding in the balm of her aunt's reassuring presence, Merry grinned. 'Your voice was in my head when I was choosing. Tailored, *structured*,' she teased, stepping into the church porch. 'Where's Angel's father? He offered to walk me down the aisle, which I thought was very kind of him.'

'Yes, quite the charmer, that man,' Sybil pronounced a shade tartly, evidently having already met Charles Russell. 'But I told him he could sit back down because I'm here now and I'll do the long walk.'

'I think you'd rather take a long walk off a plank,' Merry warned the older woman gently.

Sybil squeezed the hand she was gripping and

smiled warmly down at the young woman who
had been more her daughter than her niece, only
to stiffen nervously at the prospect of the confession that she knew she *had* to make some time
soon. Natalie had asked her to tell Merry the truth
and Sybil was now duty-bound to reveal that family secret. Sadly, telling that same truth had shattered her relationship with Natalie when Natalie
was eighteen years old and she could only hope
that it would not have the same devastating effect
on her bond with Merry and her child.

Gloriously ignorant of that approaching emotional storm, Merry smoothed down her dress,
which effortlessly delineated the high curve of her
breasts and her neat waist before falling softly to
her feet, lending her a shapely silhouette. Straightening her slight shoulders, she lifted her head high,
her short flirty veil dancing round her flushed
face, accentuating the light blue of her eyes.

Even before she went down the aisle, she heard
Elyssa chuckling. Her daughter was in the care
of her new nanny, a lovely down-to-earth young
woman from Yorkshire called Sally, who had
impressed both Merry and Angel with her genuine warmth and interest in children. Merry's
eyes skimmed from her daughter's curly head
and waving arms as she danced on Sally's knee
and settled on Angel, poised at the altar with an

equally tall dark male, Vitale, whose resemblance to Angel echoed his obvious family relationship to his brother. But Angel had the edge in Merry's biased opinion, the lean, beautiful precision of his bronzed features highlighting the shimmering brilliance of his dark eyes and his undeniable hold on her attention.

Her breath caught in her dry throat and butterflies ran amok in her tummy, her chest stretched so tightly that her lungs felt compressed. Her hand slid off Sybil's arm, suddenly nerveless as she reached the altar to be greeted by the Greek Orthodox priest. Angel gripped her cold fingers, startling her, and she glanced up at him, noticing the tension stamped in his strong cheekbones and the compressed line of his wide, sensual mouth. Yes, getting wed had to be a sheer endurance test for a wayward playboy like Angel Valtinos, Merry reflected with rueful amusement, but it was an unfortunate thought because she started wondering then whether he would find the tedious domestic aspects of family life and the unchanging nature of a wife a trial and a bore. The service marched on regardless of her teeming anxiety. The vows were exchanged, an ornately plaited gold wedding ring that she savoured for its distinctiveness and his selection of it slid onto her finger and then a matching one onto his.

And then, jolting her out of the powerful spell that Angel cast, Charles Russell surged up to her to kiss her warmly on both cheeks, closely followed by Sybil, who strove to conceal her shotgun attitude to Angel with bright, determined positivity. Elyssa, seated in a nearby pew on Sally's lap, held out her arms and wailed pathetically for her mother.

'That little chancer knows how to pick her moment,' Sybil remarked wryly as Merry bent to accept her daughter and hoisted her up, only to be intercepted by Angel, who snagged his daughter mid-manoeuvre, saying that the bride could scarcely cart a child down the aisle.

'Says who?' Merry teased, watching Elyssa pluck at his curls and his tie with nosy little hands, watching Angel suddenly slant a grin at his lack of control over the situation. Once again she found herself suppressing her surprise at his flexibility when at the mercy of a wilful baby.

Angel maintained a grip on his daughter for the handful of photos taken on the church steps. Merry watched paparazzi wield cameras behind a barrier warded by security guards, their interest visibly sharpened by her daughter's first public appearance. Her eyes widened in dismay when she finally recognised how much her life and Elyssa's were about to change. For years, Angel's every move had been fodder for the tabloid press. He had his own jet, his own yacht and the glitzy lifestyle of great wealth and privilege. His very marked degree of good looks and predilection for scantily dressed blonde beauties only added to his media appeal. Naturally his sudden marriage and the apparent existence of a young child were worthy of even closer scrutiny. Merry wondered gloomily if she would be denounced as a fertile scheming former Valtinos employee.

As they were moving towards the limousine to depart for the hotel another limo drew up ahead of them and a tiny brunette on skyrocketing heels leapt out in a flurry of colourful draperies and a feathered hat. She was as exquisite as a highly sophisticated and perfectly groomed doll. 'Oh, Charles, have I missed it?' she exclaimed very loudly while all around her cameras began to flash.

Angel murmured something very terse in Greek while his father moved off to perform the welcome that his son clearly wasn't in the mood to offer to the late-arriving guest. Angel relocated Elyssa with Sally and swept Merry into their vehicle without further ado.

'Who was that?' Merry demanded, filled with curiosity, glancing out of the window to note that the brunette was actually lodged at the security barriers exchanging comments with the paparazzi while posing like a professional. 'Is she a model or something?'

'Or something,' Angel breathed with withering impatience. 'That's Angelina.'

'Your *mother*?' Merry gasped in disbelief. 'She *can't* be! She doesn't look old enough.'

'And it's typical of her to miss the ceremony. She hates weddings,' Angel divulged. 'At a wedding the bride is the centre of attention and Angelina Valtinos cannot bear to be one of the crowd.'

Merry frowned. 'Oh, I'm sure she's not as bad as that,' she muttered, chiding him.

'No doubt you'll make your own mind up on that score,' Angel responded wryly, visibly reluctant to say any more on the topic of his mother.

'Is she likely to be the interfering mother-in-law type?' Merry prompted apprehensively.

'*Thee mou*, you have to be kidding!' Angel emitted a sharp cynical laugh. 'She couldn't care less that I've got married or who I've married but she'll be furious that I've made her a grandmother because she will see that as aging.'

Merry could not comprehend the idea of such an attitude. Sybil had approached maturity with grace, freely admitting that she found it more relaxing not to always be fretting about her appearance.

'I love the dress.' Swiftly changing the unwelcome subject, Angel enveloped Merry in a smouldering appraisal that somehow contrived to encompass the ripe swell of her breasts below the fitted bodice. 'You have a spectacular figure.'

Heat surged into Merry's cheeks at that unexpected and fairly basic compliment. His fierce appraisal emanated raw male appreciation. Her stomach performed a sudden somersault, a shard of hunger piercing her vulnerable body with the stabbing accuracy of a knife that couldn't be avoided. He could do that to her simply with a look, a tone, a smile. It always, *always* unnerved her, making her feel out of control.

The reception was being held at a five-star exclusive city hotel. Merry met her mother-in-law for the first time over the pre-dinner drinks. By then Angelina Valtinos had a young and very handsome Italian man on her arm, whom she airily introduced as Primo. She said very little, asked nothing and virtually ignored her son, as though she blamed him for the necessity of her having to attend his wedding.

'She's even worse in person than I expected,' Sybil hissed in a tone most unlike her.

'Shush…time will tell,' Merry said with a shrug.

'I wish that wretched man would take a hint,' Sybil complained as Charles Russell hurried forward with a keen smile to escort her aunt to their seats at the top table.

Merry tried not to laugh, having quickly grasped that Angel's father had one of those drivingly energetic and assured natures that steamrollered across Sybil's polite lack of interest without even noticing it. But then she had equally quickly realised that she liked her father-in-law for his unquestioning acceptance of their sudden marriage. His enthusiastic response to Elyssa had also spelled out the message that he was one of those men who absolutely adored children. He exuded all the warmth and welcome that his ex-wife, Angelina, conspicuously lacked.

Angel's brother, Prince Vitale, drifted over to exchange a few words. He was very smooth, very sophisticated and civil, but Merry was utterly intimidated by him. From the moment Angel had explained that his half-brother was of royal birth and the heir to the throne of a small, fabulously rich European country, Merry had been nervous of meeting him.

A slender blonde grasped Merry's hand and, looking up at the taller woman, Merry froze in consternation. Recognition was instant: it was the *same* blonde she had twice seen in Angel's company, a slender, leggy young woman in her early thirties with sparkling brown eyes and an easy, confident smile.

'Merry…allow me to introduce Roula Paulides, one of my oldest friends,' Angel proffered warmly.

With difficulty, Merry flashed a smile onto her stiff lips, her colour rising because she was mortified by her instant stiffening defensiveness with the other woman. An old friend, she should've thought of that possibility, she scolded herself. That more than anything else explained Angel's enduring relationship with the beautiful blonde. Unfortunately, Roula Paulides was stunning and very much Angel's type. Even worse and mortifyingly, she was the same woman who had been lunching with Angel on the dreadful dark day when Merry had had to tell him that she was pregnant.

It was only when Sally retrieved Elyssa to whisk her upstairs for a nap that Angel's mother finally approached Merry. A thin smile on her face, she said, 'Angel really should have warned me that his bride already had a child.'

'He should've done,' Merry agreed mildly.

'Your daughter is very young. Who is her father?' Angelina demanded with a ringing clarity that encouraged several heads to turn in their direction. 'I hope you are aware that she cannot make use of the Valtinos name.'

'I think you'll find you're wrong about that,' Sybil declared as she strolled over to join her niece with a protective gleam in her gaze. 'Elyssa is a Valtinos too.'

Angel's mother stiffened, her eyes widening, her rosebud mouth tightening with disbelief. 'My son has a child with you?' she gasped, stricken. 'That can't be true!'

'It is,' Merry cut in hurriedly, keen to bring the fraught conversation to an end.

'He should've married Roula... I always thought that if he married anyone, it would be Roula,' Angelina Valtinos volunteered in a tone of bitter complaint.

'Well, tact isn't one of her skills,' Sybil remarked ruefully when they were alone again. 'Who's Roula? Or don't you know?'

Merry felt humiliated by the tense little scene and her mother-in-law's closing comment about Roula Paulides. Roula, evidently, was something more than a harmless old friend, she gathered unhappily.

Meanwhile, shaken by what she had learned and very flushed, Angelina stalked to the end of the table to approach her son, who was talking to Vitale. A clearly hostile and brief dialogue took place between mother and son before the older woman careened angrily away again to snatch a glass of champagne off a passing waiter's tray and drop down into her chair.

Sybil's eyes met Merry's but neither of them commented.

'Your mother's all worked up about Elyssa,' Merry acknowledged when Angel sank fluidly down into his seat by her side. 'Why?'

'The horror of being old enough to be a grand-parent,' Angel proffered wryly.

'Are you serious?'

'There's nothing we can do about it. She'll have to learn to deal.'

'Do you see much of your mother?' Merry probed uneasily.

'More than I sometimes wish. She makes use of all my properties,' Angel admitted flatly. 'But if she wants that arrangement to continue she will have to tone herself down.'

As the afternoon wore on Merry watched Angel's mother drink like a fish and then put on a sparkling display on the dance floor with Primo. She did not behave like a woman likely to tone her extrovert nature down. Merry also saw Angelina seek out Roula Paulides and sit with the blonde for a long time while enjoying an animated conversation. So, she was unlikely to be flavour of the month with her mother-in-law any time soon, Merry told herself wryly. Well, she could live with that, she decided, secure in the circle of Angel's arms as they moved round the dance floor. His lean, powerful body against hers sparked all sorts of disconcerting responses. The prickly awareness of proximity and touch rippled through her in stormy, ever-rolling waves. She rested her head down on his shoulder, drinking in the raw, evocative scent of him like a drug she could not live without and only just resisting the urge to lick the strong brown column of his masculine throat.

Early evening, the newly married couple flew out to Greece and the Valtinos home on the island of Palos where Angel had been born. Merry was madly curious about the small island and the darkness that screened her view of it frustrated her. Serried lines of light ascending a hillside illuminated a small white village above the bay as the helicopter came in to land. A pair of SUVs picked them up, ferrying them up a steep road lined with cypress trees to the ultra-modern house hugging the promontory. Like a giant cruise ship, the entire house seemed to be lit up.

They stepped out into the warmth of a dusky evening and mounted the steps into the house. Staff greeted them in an octagonal marble hall ornamented by contemporary pieces of sculpture.

'Sally will take Elyssa straight to bed,' Angel decreed, closing his hand over Merry's before she could dart off in the wake of her daughter. 'She's so tired she'll sleep. This is *our* night.'

Merry coloured, suddenly insanely conscious of the ridiculous fact that she had barely acknowledged that it was their wedding night. She was tempted to argue that she had to take care of Elyssa, but was too well aware of their nanny's calm efficiency to tilt at windmills. Even so, because she was accustomed to being a full-time mother, she found it difficult to step back from the role and accept that someone else could do the job almost as well. Her slender fingers scrabbled indecisively in the grip of Angel's large masculine hand until she finally followed his lead and the staff already moving ahead of them with their bags.

'Supper has been prepared for us. We'll eat in our room,' Angel told her lazily. 'I'm glad to be home. You'll love it here. Midsummer it can be unbearably hot but in June Palos is lush with growth and the air is fresh.'

'I didn't realise that you were so attached to your home,' Merry confided, running her attention over the display of impressive paintings in the corridor.

'Palos has been the Valtinos base for generations,' Angel told her. 'The original house was demolished and rebuilt by my grandfather. He fancied himself as something of an architect but his design ambitions were thwarted when he and my grandmother split up and she refused to move out.

His house plan was then divided in two, one half for him, the other half for her and it's still like that. Some day I hope to turn it back into one house.'

Merry was frowning. 'Your grandparents divorced?'

'No, neither of them wanted a divorce, but after my mother's birth they separated. He was an incorrigible Romeo and she couldn't live with him,' Angel admitted as carved wooden doors were spread back at the end of the corridor. 'I never knew either of them. My grandfather didn't marry until he was almost sixty and my grandmother was in her forties when my mother was born. They died before my parents married.'

On the threshold, Merry paused to admire the magnificent bedroom. An opulent seating area took up one corner of the vast room. Various doors led off to bathroom facilities and a large and beautifully fitted dressing room where staff were already engaged in unpacking their cases. A table sat beside patio doors that led out onto a terrace overlooking a fabulous infinity swimming pool lit with underwater lights. In the centre of the room a giant bed fit for Cleopatra and draped in spicy Mediterranean colours sat on elaborate gilded feet. Her expressive face warmed, her pulses humming beneath her calm surface because she ached for him, and that awareness of her own hunger embarrassed her as nothing else could because she was mortifyingly conscious that she had no control around Angel.

'Let's eat,' Angel suggested lazily.

A slender figure clad in loose linen trousers and an emerald-green top with ties, Merry took a seat. She had dressed comfortably for the flight and had marvelled that, even in designer jeans and a black shirt, Angel could still look far more sleek and sophisticated than she did. No matter what he wore, he had that knack, if there was such a thing, of always looking classy and exclusive.

Wine was poured, the first course delivered. It was all food calculated to tempt the appetite, nothing heavy or over spiced and, because she hadn't eaten much at the wedding, Merry ate hungrily. During the main course, she heard splashing from the direction of the pool and then a sudden bout of high-pitched giggling. She began awkwardly to twist her head around to look outside.

'Diavole!' Angel swore with a sudden frown, flying upright to thrust open the doors onto the terrace.

Merry rose to her feet more slowly and followed him to see what had jerked him out of his seat as though rudely yanked up by invisible steel wires. She was very much taken aback to discover that the source of the noise was her mother-in-law and

her boyfriend, both of whom appeared to be ca-
vorting naked in the pool. She blinked in disbelief
while Angel addressed the pair in angry Greek.
Primo reacted first, hauling himself hurriedly out
of the water and yanking a towel off a lounger to
wind it round his waist. Angelina hissed back at
her son in furious Greek before leaving the pool
by the steps, stark naked and evidently quite unconcerned by that reality. Her companion strode
forward to toss her a robe, his discomfiture at the
interruption unhidden. Angel's mother, however,
took her time about covering up, her tempestuous
fury at Angel's intrusion fuelling a wealth of outraged objections.

Merry swallowed hard on her growing embarrassment while Angel stood his ground, his dark
deep voice sardonic and clipped with derision as
he switched to English. 'You will not use this pool
while I, my wife or my daughter are in residence.'

'This is my home!' Angelina proclaimed. 'You
have no right to make a demand like that!'

'This house belongs to me and there are now
rules to be observed,' Angel sliced back harshly.
'If you cannot respect those rules, find somewhere
else to stay on the island.'

And with that final ringing threat, Angel swung
back and pressed a hand to Merry's shoulder to
guide her firmly back indoors. His mother ranted

back at him in Greek and he ignored the fact, ramming shut the doors again and returning to their interrupted meal.

Unnerved by what she had witnessed, Merry dropped heavily back into her chair, her face hot with unease. 'I think your mother's had too much to drink.'

Angel shot her a grim glance. 'Don't make excuses for her. I should have told her that she was no longer welcome here *before* we married. Her conduct is inappropriate and I refuse to have you or Elyssa subjected to her behaviour in what is now your home.'

Merry sipped at her wine, stunned by the display she had witnessed and wondering helplessly what it had been like for him to grow up with so avant-garde a mother. Angelina seemed to have no boundaries, no concept of what was acceptable. It must have been a nightmare to grow up in the care of so self-indulgent a woman. For the first time she understood why Angel was so close to his father: he only had one parent, he had only *ever* had one parent. Parenting had been something that Angelina Valtinos had probably never done and she understood why Angel had been placed in a boarding school at a very young age.

As silence reclaimed the pool beyond the terrace, Angel audibly expelled his breath, the fierce tension in his lean, darkly handsome features and the set of his wide shoulders fading. He was determined that Merry would not be embarrassed by his mother's attention-grabbing tactics. Merry was too prim to comfortably cope with the scenes his mother liked to throw. In any case, his wife was entitled to the older woman's respect. Angelina could dislike her all she wished but, ultimately, she had to accept that her son's wife was the new mistress of the house and had the right to expect certain standards of behaviour.

'How is it that the family home belongs to you and not to your mother?' Merry asked curiously.

'My grandmother survived my grandfather by several months. She was never able to control her daughter and once she realised that Angelina was pregnant, she left this house to my mother's descendants rather than to her,' he advanced.

Merry frowned. 'That's kind of sad.'

'Don't feel sorry for Angelina. My grandfather adored her and endowed her with a massive trust fund. All her life she has done exactly what she wanted to do, regardless of how it harms or affects others. At some stage, there's got to be a price to pay for that,' Angel declared with dry finality. 'I have long wished that my mother would buy her own property where she could do as she likes without involving me.'

'Why doesn't she do that?' Merry asked with genuine curiosity.

'The ownership of property involves other responsibilities. Hiring staff, maintenance, running costs…all the adult stuff,' he pointed out with a sardonic twist of his wide, sensual mouth. 'My mother avoids responsibility of any kind. May we drop this subject?'

'Of course,' Merry conceded, a little breathless while she collided with smouldering dark eyes and sipped at her wine. Her mind, however, remained awash with conjecture about her mother-in-law and her disconnected and antagonistic relationship with her son. At the same time she wasn't worried about Angelina causing trouble between them because she could see that Angel had few illusions about his parent and intended to protect her from any fallout. And that made her a little sad, made her wonder what it must have been like for him to be saddled with a spoilt heiress of a mother, a party girl, who flatly refused to accept responsibility and grow up. A mother who, from what she could see, had never behaved like a normal mother. Surely that truth must've lessened his respect for women and his ability to trust her sex, she reasoned helplessly.

'Let's concentrate on us,' Angel suggested with emphatic cool.

She felt overheated and her mouth ran dry. Her entire body tensed, tiny little tremors shimmying through her pelvis, tremors of awareness, arousal and anticipation. She was embarrassed by the level of her sheer susceptibility, shaken by the power he had over her, suddenly wondering if he too knew the full extent of it…

CHAPTER SEVEN

ANGEL GRASPED HER HAND and eased her up out of her seat. 'I have a special request,' he admitted almost harshly.

Enthralled by the golden glimmer of his intense appraisal, Merry moistened her dry lips with the tip of her tongue. 'And what would that be?'

Long fingers flicked the silken bell of hair that fell to just below her shoulders. 'You cut your hair. I loved it the way it was. Will you grow it again for me?' he asked levelly.

Surprise darted through Merry, who had wondered if he had even noticed that she had shortened her hair. 'I suppose that could be arranged,' she breathed shakily.

'Why did you cut it?' he demanded. 'It was really beautiful.'

Even more taken aback by that blunt question and the compliment, Merry coloured. She couldn't tell him the truth, couldn't afford to dwell on unfortunate memories at this stage of their marriage or mention truths that he might think were aimed at reproaching him. But when she had been pregnant and struggling against an unending tide of exhaustion and sickness to get through every day, the amount of care demanded by very long hair had simply felt like an unnecessary burden.

'It was too much work to look after when I was pregnant,' she muttered awkwardly.

'Fortunately, you no longer have to look after your own hair,' Angel informed her lazily. 'Add a stylist to your staff—'

Merry opened pale blue eyes very wide. 'I'm to have my own staff?' she gasped.

'Of course. You'll need a social secretary to take care of your calendar, someone to shop for you…unless you want to do it yourself,' Angel volunteered doubtfully. 'I've started you off with a new wardrobe—'

'Have you indeed?' Merry cut in jerkily.

'It's a wedding present. I wasn't sure you'd want to be bothered,' Angel volunteered, a fingertip tracing the quivering fullness of her lower lip, sending a shiver through her taut, slender body. 'You've never struck me as being that interested in clothes or appearances.'

'I'm not,' she agreed almost guiltily. 'Sybil was

always trying to persuade me that shopping was enjoyable.'

'I don't want you having to do things you don't want to do,' Angel told her huskily. 'I don't want you to change who you are to fit into my world, so it's easier to have someone else take care of the less welcome aspects for you.'

Her heartbeat was thumping hard and fast inside her tightening chest. 'You like me the way I am?'

'Very much,' Angel asserted. 'You're unusual and I value that.'

A smile slowly tilted and softened the tense line of her mouth. 'And you have a fetish for very long hair?'

A wolfish grin slashed his expressive mouth, cutting his dark male beauty into high-cheekboned perfection and interesting hollows while his intense gaze held hers fast. 'Only from the first moment I saw you.'

Warmth flushed through Merry, leaving her breathless. 'That must be the most romantic thing you've ever said to me.'

'I don't do romantic, *koukla mou*,' Angel told her uneasily, a frown line building between his fine ebony brows as he stared down at her in frustration. 'For me, it was a sexual charge and instantaneous...'

And if she was honest, Merry reflected ruefully, it had been the same for her that first day, a powerful instant physical reaction that had only deepened with repeated exposure.

Lean brown hands dropped to the sash at her waist and jerked it loose so that her breath hitched in her throat. She could feel her breasts swelling inside her bra, her nipples prickling into feverish prominence, the sense of melting at her feminine core. She was trembling, awake on every level even before he picked her up against him and crushed her ripe mouth hungrily under his.

'*Thee mou...* I want you even more now than I wanted you then,' Angel intoned rawly. 'And that's saying something. But then I've never had to be patient before.'

'You don't have any patience,' she whispered through reddened lips. 'You want everything yesterday.'

'Once I got you back I didn't want to be too demanding in case it made you change your mind. Before the wedding, I felt like I was in a straitjacket around you, forced to be on my best behaviour,' he complained.

Merry laughed, riveted to appreciate that she had read his uncharacteristic restraint correctly. She knew him better than she had believed, she thought victoriously, and his admission thrilled her. He hadn't wanted to risk driving her away and losing her. Losing *them*, she corrected with a sudden inner flinch of dismayed acceptance, the thrilled sensation swiftly dying again. He had practised patience with Elyssa's mother for Elyssa's benefit, fearful of losing access through their marriage to his daughter, which put a very different slant on his attitude.

'Unhappily for me, I am a naturally demanding man,' Angel admitted thickly, long, deft fingers twitching the buttons loose on her top, parting the edges, pushing them off her slim, taut shoulders until the garment dropped to the tiled floor. 'No good at waiting, no fan of deferred gratification either…'

Her ribcage tensed as she snatched in a sustaining breath, ridiculously self-conscious standing there in her simple white lace bra. Although they had been intimate twice before, on the first occasion they had been in semi-darkness and on the second they had both been so frantic that she hadn't had the time or space to feel remotely shy. But now, her face burned as Angel released the catch on her bra and her breasts tumbled free, plump and swollen and heavy.

'I have died and gone to heaven,' Angel intoned, scooping her up and carrying her across to the bed. 'I love your curves.'

'I'm pretty much stuck with them,' Merry

pointed out, resisting a very strong urge to cup
her hands over the swells that pregnancy had in-
creased in size.

Angel cupped the burgeoning creamy swells,
gently moulded and stroked them before leaning
back to peel his shirt off over his head. Tangled
black curls, glossy below the discreet lights, tumbled over his brow, his lean, strong face taut with
hunger, dark golden eyes glittering like polished
ingots. A thumb teased a quivering pink nipple
until it hardened into a tight bud and throbbed, her
breath escaping from her parted lips in an audible
hiss of quaking response.

'You *should* tremble… I want to eat you alive,'
Angel warned her, settling his hands to her waist
to extract her from her linen trousers, yanking
them off with scant ceremony and trailing off her
last garment with brazen satisfaction. 'But we've
never taken the time to do this properly. We were
always in a ridiculous hurry to reach the finishing
line. It won't be like that tonight.'

Merry felt the dampness between her thighs
and reddened fiercely, wildly aware that her body
was even now ready for him, surging impatiently
ahead without shame to that finishing line he
had mentioned. He made her single-minded and
greedy and shameless, she thought helplessly. He
turned everything she thought she knew about

herself on its head and he had done that from the outset.

Watching her, Angel sprang upright again to strip off what remained of his clothes. He was, oh, so beautiful that she stared, taking in the long, bronzed flexing torso lightly sprinkled with black curling hair, the superb muscle definition, the long, powerful, hair-roughened thighs and the bold, eager thrust of his erection. Her belly fluttered, her mouth ran dry, her body flexed with sinful eagerness.

He returned to her again, all smouldering sexual assurance and with eyes that ravished her as she lay there. His hands found her curvy hips, his mouth locked to a rosy crest, and she simply gasped while he played with the puckered buds until they throbbed almost unbearably. A finger trailed through her slick folds and her spine arched, another sound, a plea for more that she couldn't help, dragged from her. He spread her thighs to invade her body with skilful fingers and slid down her pale body to explore her most tender flesh.

Merry was already so aroused that she could barely contain herself. He toyed with her, brought his mouth to her and licked and teased until she writhed helplessly beneath his ministrations, her body alight like a forest fire, hot and twitchy and excited beyond bearing. It was as though every nerve ending had reached saturation point, thrusting her higher and higher with every passing second until her body shattered in an ecstatic climax without her volition. A high keening cry fell from her, her body jerking and gasping with the intensity of her relief as the long, convulsive waves of pleasure rippled through her again.

'You really needed that,' Angel husked knowingly, his brilliant gaze locked to her hectically flushed and softened face. 'So did I. I needed to see you come for me again. I need to know I'm the only man to see you like this.'

'Why?' she asked baldly, taken aback by that admission.

Angel shrugged a broad shoulder. 'I don't know,' he admitted, quite unconcerned by his own ignorance of what motivated him. 'But when I saw you kissing that vet guy I wanted to wipe him off the face of the earth.'

Merry sat up with a start and hugged her knees in consternation. 'How did you see that?'

'You and Elyssa have had a security detail discreetly watching over you for months. It's standard in this family and not negotiable,' Angel told her without apology. 'I needed to know you were both safe. I was sent a photo of you kissing him. I didn't need to see that. I didn't ask for it. I hated it.'

Merry sat there frozen, shock and resentment

momentarily holding her fast. 'Standard?' she queried.

'It's my job to keep you both safe,' he delivered flatly. 'But sometimes you don't want the details. Did you have sex with him?'

'None of your business!' Merry framed jaggedly, swinging her legs off the bed and standing up. 'How many women have you been with since the night Elyssa was conceived?'

The silence simmered like a kettle suddenly pushed close to noisy boiling point.

Merry swung back to him, too angry to even care that she was naked. 'I thought that would shut you up!'

'After our little contraceptive mishap it was months before I was with anyone again. I couldn't get you or that accident out of my head. I still wanted you but I *had* to stay away from you,' Angel ground out with suppressed savagery, his lean, dark features rigid with remembered frustration and resentment. 'Every other woman turned me off. You destroyed my sex drive until I got very, very drunk one night and finally broke the dry spell.'

Well, that was blunt and very Angel brutal, Merry acknowledged, stalking into the bathroom with hot stinging tears brimming in her eyes. And she still wanted to kill him, rake jealous fingernails down over his beautiful face and draw blood in punishment. Jealousy and hatred ate her alive, threatening to rip her asunder because she had no defence against such honesty. Of course, she had guessed there would be other women, other flings and sexual dalliances while they were apart, but guessing and *knowing* were two very different things.

Inside the bathroom, Angel closed two strong arms round her to hold her fast. 'It was the worst sex I've ever had.'

'Good!' she bit out with raw sincerity.

'It wasn't like you and me. It wasn't what I really wanted but I couldn't *have* what I wanted and celibacy made me feel like a weakling,' he groaned against the damp nape of her neck. 'The sexual hold you had over me unnerved me right from the beginning. It felt toxic, dangerous…'

'Thanks… I think,' Merry framed weakly as he wrapped his strong arms even more tightly round her, imprisoning her in the hard, damp heat of his lean, powerful body.

'It was the same for you. You fought it as well,' he reminded her.

And that was true, she conceded grudgingly. That overpowering hunger had scared her, overwhelmed her, made her all too aware of her vulnerability. Could it really have been the same for him?

'Even if the condom hadn't broken that night, I'd have run like a hare,' Angel admitted in a driven undertone. 'I felt out of control. I couldn't live like that.'

'Neither could I,' she confessed unevenly.

'But now that I've got that ring on your finger, everything feels different,' Angel stated, his breath fanning her shoulder, his hands smoothing up her body in innate celebration of the possessiveness roaring through him. 'You're mine now, *all* mine.'

'Am I?' she dared.

An appreciative laugh vibrated through him and his hands swept up over her breasts, moulding the ripe swells, tugging at the still-distended peaks, sending a piercing arrow of sweet shuddering sensation right down to the moist heart of her. 'If you don't know that yet, I'm doing something very wrong,' he growled, lifting her off her feet to carry her back into the bedroom.

'You have a one-track mind, Mr Valtinos,' Merry condemned helplessly as he spread her on the bed and hovered over her body, brazenly eager for more action.

'No, I have a wife to claim,' Angel declared urgently, sliding between her slender thighs, gathering them up and plunging into her with ravenous sexual dominance. 'And tonight nothing will keep me from you. Not my mistakes, not my clumsy efforts to make amends, not your disappointment in me, not my inability to live up to your impossibly high ideals. We are married and we will do the best we can with that challenge.'

His sudden intrusion into her honeyed depths stretched her tight and then sent a current of melting excitement surging through Merry. She closed her eyes as he moved, her head falling back, her body an erotic instrument in his charge, glorious sensation spilling through her, washing away the hurt and the disillusionment. Oh, later she would take out the hurt again and brood on it and hate herself, but just then she couldn't hold onto that pain, not when a delicious flood of exquisite feeling clenched her core with his every sensual movement. He felt like hers for the first time, and as an explosive orgasm lit her up from inside out and he groaned with passionate pleasure into her hair she was soothed, quieted and gratified to be the source of that uninhibited satisfaction.

CHAPTER EIGHT

MERRY AND ANGEL lay side by side in the orange grove above the private beach. Day after day had melted into the next with a curiously timeless quality that had gradually teased all the tension from Merry's bones and taught her how to relax. She could hardly credit that they had already spent an entire month on the island. Her body ached from his demands, not that she wasn't willing, but she was still in shock at the extent of Angel's ravenous hunger for her.

It was sex, only sex, she told herself regularly, and then in the dark of the night when Angel wasn't his sardonic know-all self she snuggled up to him, revelling in the intimacy that now bonded them. Maintaining a controlled distance wasn't possible with a man as unashamedly physical as the one she had married. Angel had no limits. He would go and work for a couple of hours in his home office and then sweep down on her wherever she was and cart her off to bed again as if he had been parted from her for at least a month.

'I missed you,' he would say, replete with satisfaction while her pulses still pounded and her body hummed in the aftermath.

'I could work *with* you,' she would say.

'You're my wife, the mother of my child, no longer an employee.'

'I could be a junior partner,' she had proffered pathetically.

'We can't live in each other's pockets twenty-four-seven,' Angel had pointed out drily. 'It would be unhealthy.'

No, what Merry sometimes thought was unhealthy was the sheer weight of love that Angel now inspired in her. That was a truth she had evaded as long as possible: she *loved* him.

Only because she loved him and her daughter had she been willing to give Angel one last chance, she acknowledged ruefully. There were still a thousand things she wanted to punish him for, but she knew that vengeful, bitter thoughts were unproductive and would ultimately damage any hope of their having a stable relationship. In that line, she was sensible, very sensible, she acknowledged ruefully. Unfortunately, she only became stupid when it came to Angel himself.

Sometimes she had to work uncomfortably hard

to hide her love. She would see him laughing over
Elyssa's antics in the bath, amusement lightening
and softening his lean, darkly handsome features,
and she wouldn't be able to drag her eyes from
him. He had taken her down to the village *taverna*
above the harbour and dined with her there, intro-
ducing her to the locals, more relaxed than she had
ever seen him in company, his usually razor-edged
cynicism absent. He had tipped her out of bed to
climb the highest hill on the island to see in the
dawn and told her off for moaning about how tired
she was even though he had drained her energy at
the summit with *al fresco* sex. But of course she
was tired, making love half the night and half the
day, physically active in all the hours between as
she strove to match his high-voltage energy levels.

Ironically, complete peace had engulfed the
Valtinos house the day after the wedding once
Angel had revealed that his mother and her boyfriend had departed at dawn for an unknown des-
tination, leaving the other half of the house in a
fine mess for the staff to deal with. Merry had
felt relieved and then guilty at feeling relieved because, like it or not, Angel's challenging and difficult mother was family and had to somehow be
integrated into their lives or become a continuing
problem.

They had gone sailing on the yacht, visiting

other islands, shopping, picnicking. They had thrown a giant party at the house attended by all Angel's relatives, near and distant. She had met his second cousin who lived in London and had heard all about Angel's visit to her home before he first met Elyssa, and Merry had laughed like a drain when she'd recognised how wily he had been to find out a little more about babies before he'd served himself up as a new father to one.

'What's your favourite colour?' she asked drowsily.

'I'm not a girl. I don't have a favourite,' Angel parried with amusement.

'Birth sign?'

'Look at your marriage certificate, lazy-bones,' he advised. 'I'm a Scorpio, but I don't believe in that sh—'

'Language,' she reminded him, resting a finger against his parted lips.

'Prim, proper, prissy,' Angel labelled without hesitation.

'Your first lover? What age were you?' she pressed, defying that censure while wondering how on earth he could still think of her that way after the time they had spent together.

'Too young. You don't want to know,' Angel traded.

'I *do* want to know,' Merry argued, stretching

indolently in the drenching heat, only vaguely wondering what time it was. They had spent the morning swimming and entertaining Elyssa on the beach and then Sally had come down to collect their daughter and take her back up to the house for lunch and a nap. Now the surf was whispering onto the shore a hundred yards below them while the cane forest that sheltered the orange grove from the coastal breezes concealed them entirely from view.

'I was fourteen. She was one of my mother's friends,' Angel admitted grimly.

Frowning, Merry flipped over to stare at him. *'Seriously?'*

'You're still so naïve,' Angel groaned, lifting up on his elbows to study her, hard muscles flexing on his bare bronzed torso, the vee at his hipbones prominent above the low-slung shorts as he leant back. Just looking at that display of stark masculine beauty made her mouth run dry and her heart give a sudden warning thud, awareness thundering through her at storm-force potency.

'What do you think it was like here when I was an adolescent with Angelina in charge?' he chided. 'I came home for the summer from school and there were no rules whatsoever. Back then it was all wild, decadent parties and the house was awash with people. Believe it or not, my mother was even less inhibited in those days and, being an oversexed teenager, I naturally thought the free-dom to do anything I liked was amazing and I never let my father know how debauched it was.'

'So, your first experience was with an older woman,' Merry gathered, determined to move on past that sordid revelation and not judge, because when he had been that young and innocent she believed he had been more sinned against than he had been a sinner.

'And the experience was disappointing,' Angel admitted with derisive bite. 'It felt sleazy, not em-powering. I felt used. When the parties here got too much I used to go down and camp out with Roula's family for a few days.'

'She lived here on the island back then?' Merry said in surprise.

'Still does. Roula was born and bred on Palos, like me. This is her home base too. She runs a chain of beauty salons, comes back here for a break. Un-like me, she had a regular family with parents who were still married and their home was a little oasis of peace and normality... I loved escaping there,' he confided. 'Rules and regular meal times have more appeal than you would appreciate.'

'I can understand that,' Merry conceded rue-fully. 'My mother was very disorganised. She'd want to eat and there'd be nothing in the fridge. She'd want to go out and she wouldn't have a babysitter arranged. Sometimes she just left me in bed and went out anyway. I never told Sybil that. But when I was with Sybil, everything was structured.'

'*Thee mou…* I forgot!' Angel exclaimed abruptly. 'Your aunt phoned to ask me if there was any chance we'd be back in the UK in the next couple of weeks because your mother's coming over to stay with her for a while and she wants to see you. I said I'd try to organise it.'

Merry frowned, reluctant to get on board with yet another reconciliation scene with her estranged mother. Natalie enjoyed emotional scenes, enjoyed asking her daughter why she couldn't act more like a normal daughter and love and appreciate her, not seeming to realise that the time for laying the foundation for such bonds lay far behind them. They had missed that boat and Merry had learned to get by without a mother by replacing her with the more dependable Sybil.

'You're not keen,' Angel gathered, shrewd dark golden eyes scanning her expressive troubled face. 'Sybil made it sound like it was really important that you show up at some stage. I think she's hoping you'll mend fences with her sister.'

Merry shrugged jerkily. 'I've tried before and it never worked. Sybil's a peacemaker and wants everyone to be happy but I always annoy Natalie by saying or doing the wrong thing.'

'Try giving her another chance,' Angel urged, surprising her. 'I don't get on with my mother either, but then she doesn't make any effort to get on with me. At least yours is willing to make the effort.'

'And when it goes pear-shaped, she blames me every time,' Merry said bitterly.

'You can be an unforgiving little soul when people fail your high expectations,' Angel murmured softly. 'I know you haven't forgiven me yet for running out on you.'

Her face froze. 'What makes you think that?'

'Be honest. I'm still on probation. You're always waiting for me to do something dreadful and show my true colours,' Angel told her impatiently. 'You hold back. You watch everything you say and do and always give me the carefully sanitised version.'

Merry clashed in shock with hot dark golden eyes and recognised his exasperation. Guilty dismay pierced her and she was even more taken aback by how very clearly he saw through her pretences to her fearful desire to keep the peace. He lifted a hand and traced the full, soft curve of her lower lip as she caught it between her teeth.

'I don't mean to be like that,' she admitted uncomfortably.

'I'll have to work that pessimistic streak out of

you. By all means, set the bar high because I do rise to a challenge,' Angel assured her. 'But don't drown me before I can even begin in low expectations.'

'I *don't* have low expectations,' Merry protested breathlessly, flipping over to face him, her colour high.

Angel grasped her hand and spread her fingers low on his belly with a glittering smile of disagreement. 'Go on, tell me you're too tired or just not in the mood for once,' he urged.

Her small fingers flexed against his sun-warmed skin and then pulled defiantly free to trace the furrow of silky hair that ran down from his navel to vanish beneath the waistband of his shorts. Heat uncoiled and spread low in her belly. 'You don't get it, do you?' she whispered, flicking loose the first metal stud separating her from him. 'No matter how tired, I can't help always being in the mood for you,' she confided unsteadily. 'It's not fake, it's not me trying to please.'

She heard the startled catch of his expelled breath as she attacked the remaining studs, felt too the hardness of the arousal he couldn't possibly hide from her and she thrilled at his unashamed need for her. She had assumed that initial enthusiasm would die a death once she was no longer a novelty in his bed but he hadn't flagged in the slightest. She jerked the shorts down and reached for him.

Angel watched her in fascination. Here she was again taking him by surprise, defying his own expectations with a bold counter-attack, despite her inexperience. And he treasured her ability to disconcert him, revelling in the reality that she appeared to have more interest in his body than she had in the new wardrobe he had bought for her. She was quite unlike any other woman he had ever been with, gloriously unimpressed by his wealth and what he could buy her. Her shy fingers found him, stroked him and the sweet swell of shattering pleasure washed over him. His breath hissed out between his even white teeth. He lay back, giving her control without hesitation.

Merry licked the long, strong column of him, swiping with her tongue, eager to return the favour of his attention even if it meant she delivered a less than polished performance. The muscles on his abdomen rippled, his tension building, his hips rising as a sexy sound of reaction escaped his parted lips and she smiled, loving his responsiveness, his unexpected willingness to let her take charge for a change. She closed him between her lips and he groaned out loud, long fingers knotting into her hair, urging her on, controlling the rhythm.

'Enough!' Angel bit out abruptly, pulling her

back and slotting her deftly under him, rearranging her for what he really wanted and needed.

Splayed beneath him starfish-mode, Merry cried out as he plunged straight into her, all ferocious urgency and unleashed passion, his lean hips rising and falling between her slender thighs to send jolt after jolt of hot, sweet pleasure surging in waves through her. Her excitement climbed exponentially and when he flipped her over onto her knees and slammed into her again and again while the ball of his thumb stroked against her, he sent her flying into an explosive orgasm that left her sobbing for breath and control in the aftermath.

'No, that definitely wasn't fake or you trying to please me,' Angel murmured with roughened satisfaction in her ear as he gently tugged her hair back from her hot face and planted a lingering kiss there.

At some stage of the night, Angel shook her awake and her eyes flew open to focus on him in drowsy surprise. He was already fully dressed, sheathed in a sleek business suit, freshly shaven. He sank down on the side of the bed. 'I'm heading back to London. There's a stock-market crisis and I prefer to handle it on the spot with my staff around me. I've made arrangements for you to fly back first thing tomorrow morning…you need your sleep right now,' he said, stroking her cheekbone with unexpected tenderness. 'Once you've seen your aunt and your mother you can come and join me.'

Angel stared down at his wife, more than a little unnerved by the guilt sweeping him when he noticed the shadows below her eyes and the weary droop of her eyelids. He had been too demanding. He couldn't get enough of her in or out of bed and she was so busy being the perfect wife and perfect mother that she wasn't taking time out for her own needs. He was selfish, had always been selfish, was trying in fits and starts to be less selfish, but when he wanted her with him it was a challenge to defy his own need. Leaving her to sleep the night through was a sacrifice when he would sooner have had her by his side.

'It drives me mad when you make decisions for me!' Merry groaned in frustration. 'I could have flown back with you.'

'It wouldn't be fair to take Elyssa out of bed in the middle of the night and you're already tired out. I suggest that you leave her here with Sally unless you're planning to stay with your family for a few days,' Angel opined with an ebony brow rising in question on that score.

Merry sighed, unenthusiastic about the prospect

of seeing her mother again. 'Not very likely. After a couple of hours catching up I'll probably be glad to escape,' she forecast ruefully.

Angel sprang upright again, all lithe, sexy elegance and energy, holding her gaze like a live flame burning in the darkness. 'And I'll be glad to have you back,' he declared with a flashing smile that tilted her heart inside her and made her senses hum.

Merry recalled that brief snatch of dialogue over coffee on the terrace the following morning. It was Sally's day off and Elyssa had just gone upstairs for her nap, leaving her mother free to relax in the sunshine. She smoothed a hand down over the bright red sundress she wore, preventing it from creeping any further up her slender thighs because she didn't want to flash the gardener engaged in trimming the edges of the lawn.

Angel had bought her a new wardrobe and it had very much his stamp on it. She thought the hemlines were too short, the necklines too revealing or snug in fit and the colour choices too bold, but then she wasn't used to showing off her figure or seeking attention. Maybe that had been Angel's nefarious plan all along, she reflected with wry amusement; maybe he hoped to drive her out shopping by landing her with a selection of garments she considered too daring. She certainly wouldn't put such scheming past him. The lingerie, however, was a superb fit and very much to her taste, plain and comfortable rather than provocative or elaborate.

One of the maids walked onto the terrace to announce a visitor and a moment later Roula Paulides strolled out to join Merry, a wide smile of greeting pinned to her beautiful face. 'I heard Angel's helicopter taking off during the night and thought this would be a good opportunity for us to get better acquainted,' she admitted.

Determined to look welcoming, Merry smiled and ordered fresh coffee. Roula was one of Angel's most long-standing friends yet Merry was also conscious of the possessive vibe that flared through her whenever she relived how she had once felt seeing her husband in the glamorous blonde's company.

Roula took a seat, very self-assured in her designer casuals, her blonde hair secured in a stylish twist, her brown eyes bright as she smiled again. And something about that second smile warned Merry that her visitor wasn't half as relaxed as she was trying to appear.

'I want to make it clear that I won't make a habit of visiting like this,' Roula assured her smoothly as she lifted her coffee cup. 'We're both entitled to our privacy. We'll only occasionally meet when

Angel holds a big party because that is the only time he invites me to his home.'

'You're welcome to visit any time you like,' Merry responded easily, wondering if, in a round-about, devious way, she was being accused of being a jealous, possessive wife likely to resent and distrust any female friend of her husband's.

'Oh, that wouldn't do. Angel wouldn't allow that,' Roula declared. 'He wouldn't consider that appropriate in the circumstances. I thought he would've mentioned our arrangement by now but, although he never justifies his lifestyle, he's like most men: keen to avoid conflict.'

Merry's eyes had steadily widened throughout that speech as she struggled to work out what the other woman was talking about. 'What arrange-ment?' she heard herself ask baldly. 'I'm afraid I don't know what you're referring to.'

Roula Paulides settled cynically amused brown eyes on her. 'I'm Angel's mistress. I have been for years.'

For a split second, Merry didn't believe that she had heard that announcement because it struck her like a blow, freezing her brain into incredulous in-activity, leaving her staring back at her companion in blank disbelief.

Roula lifted and dropped a thin shoulder in acknowledgement. 'It's how he lives and I have never been able to refuse Angel anything. If you and I can reach an accommodation that we can both live with, all our lives will run much more smoothly. I'm not the jealous type and I hope you aren't either.'

Merry sucked in a shuddering breath. 'Let me get this straight. You came here today to tell me that you're sleeping with my husband?'

'Oh, not recently. Angel has no need of me right now with a new wife in his bed,' the Greek woman declared drily. 'But in time, when you are no longer a novelty, he will return to me. Other women have always come and gone in his life. I accept that. I've *always* accepted that and if you are wise and wish to remain his wife you will accept it too. You can't own him, you can't cage him.'

Merry looked beyond Roula, unnerved by the sudden throbbing intensity of her low-pitched voice and the brash, hard confidence with which she spoke, the suggestion that *she* knew Angel better than anyone else. On the hill above the village sat the Paulides home, a rather boxy modern white villa, which Angel had casually identified as being where Roula lived. Shock was winging through Merry in giddy waves of increasingly desperate denial, her fingers curling into defensive claws on her lap. It couldn't be true, it couldn't possibly be true that Angel had some permanent, non-exclusive sexual arrangement with the other woman that he had remained silent about.

'You seem shocked, but why? We were child-hood friends and have always been very close. We understand each other very well,' Roula told her calmly. 'In the same way I accepted that after your child was born, Angel would inevitably end up marrying you. He doesn't love you any more than he loves me but he will do his duty by his daughter. I'm here now only to assure you that I will never try to interfere in your marriage in any way and that I hope you will not be spiteful and try to prevent Angel from seeing me.'

Merry swallowed hard at that unlikely hope. 'What's in this weird arrangement for you?' she asked bluntly.

Roula vented a laugh and tossed her head. 'I have a share of him. I'm willing to settle for that. I've loved him since I was a girl. He rescued my father from bankruptcy and financed the set-up of my beauty salons. When I was younger I hoped that he would eventually see me as a possible wife, but of course that hasn't happened. Marrying the mistress isn't in the Valtinos genes.'

Nausea stirred in Merry's tummy. Swallowing her coffee without choking on it was a challenge. Roula managed to make it all sound so normal, so inevitable. She loved Angel, unashamedly did what it took to hold onto her small stake in his life while accepting that there would be other women and eventually a wife she would have to share him with.

But such acceptance was nowhere within Merry's grasp. She was an all-or-nothing person. She had told Angel before she agreed to marry him that he could have no other women in his life and that she expected complete fidelity. He had agreed to that boundary. Had he lied? Had he expected her to change her mind? Or had he been planning to be so discreet that she never found out that he sometimes slept with Roula Paulides?

Shock banging through her blitzed brain, Merry struggled to relocate her reasoning powers. Did she simply accept that the blonde was telling her the truth? Why would Roula lie about such a relationship? Could she simply be trying to cause trouble in Merry's marriage? But what would be the point of that unless she was already engaged in an affair with Angel with something to gain from his marriage breaking down?

And then, according to Roula, Angel had not been *with* her recently? Or simply since his marriage? Merry's head was spinning. She wanted to pack her bags, gather up her daughter and run back to the UK to establish a sane and normal life where a blonde beauty did not calmly stroll into her home one morning to announce that she was in love with Merry's husband and keen to continue having hassle-free sex with him.

Stark pain sliced through Merry, cutting through the numbness of shock. She had been happy, she registered wretchedly, hopelessly, helplessly happy with Angel and their marriage as it was. She had seen nothing to question, nothing to rouse her suspicions. She had believed his promise of fidelity, believed that they had a future, but if she believed Roula her future with Angel could only be a deceitful and fragile farce because she would never ever accept him betraying her with another woman. Nor would she ever share him.

'Well, you've said your piece. Now I think you should leave,' Merry told Roula quietly, her self-discipline absolute because wild horses could not have dredged a more vulnerable reaction from her.

'I do hope I haven't upset you,' the Greek woman said unconvincingly. 'I suspected you didn't know and that wasn't right.'

As far as Merry was concerned there was nothing right about Roula's attitude to either Angel or his marriage or even his wife. Roula had developed her own convictions based on what she wanted. Roula, it seemed, lived to please Angel. Merry loved Angel but she had never been blind to his flaws. Had he discounted his intimate relationship with Roula in the same way as he had once ignored the reality that his pregnant former employee might need more than financial support from him?

It would have been uncomfortable for Angel to overcome his own feelings back then and offer Merry his support, and he had been unable to force himself to go that extra mile for her benefit. In the same way being honest about his relationship with Roula would have put paid to any hope of Merry marrying him and sharing their daughter. Was that why he had kept quiet? Or was it possible that he believed the relationship with Roula was at an end? But then wouldn't Roula know that? Had Angel lied to Merry to get her to the altar? Was he that ruthless?

Oh, yes, a little voice chimed inside her head.

CHAPTER NINE

'Mrs Valtinos insisted that she had to make an immediate departure from the airport,' Angel's driver repeated uneasily. 'I did tell her that you were expecting her to join you for lunch before she left London but she said—'

'That she didn't have time,' Angel slotted in flatly.

'I took her to Foxcote Hall at two and then an hour later dropped her off at her aunt's house. She said she'd call when she needed to be picked up again,' the older man completed.

Angel breathed in slow and deep. Something was wrong. His wife had flown back to London with their daughter and mounds of luggage even though she had only been expecting to remain in the UK for forty-eight hours at most. She had blown him off for lunch. She wasn't answering his calls or his texts. Such behaviour was unlike her. Merry wasn't moody or facetious and she didn't play games. If something had annoyed her, she was more likely to speak up straight away. His growing bewilderment was starting to give way to righteous anger and an amount of unfamiliar apprehension that only enraged him more.

What could possibly have happened between his departure and her arrival in London? Why the mounds of luggage? Wasn't she planning to return to Greece? Was it possible that she was leaving him and taking their daughter with her? But why would she do that? He had checked with the staff on Palos. Merry had had only one visitor and that was Roula, and when he had phoned Roula she had insisted that Merry had been perfectly friendly and relaxed with her. His lean brown hands knotting into fists, his tension pronounced, Angel resolved to be waiting at Foxcote when Merry got back.

Merry emerged from the rambling country house that she had not until that day known that Angel owned and climbed into the waiting limousine. She had left Elyssa with Sally, deeming it unlikely that her mother was likely to be champing at the bit to meet her first grandchild because Natalie had never had much time for babies. Furthermore, if Natalie was likely to be chastising her daughter and creating one of her emotionally exhausting scenes it was better to keep Elyssa well away from the display because Merry always lost patience with the older woman. What did it matter after all these years anyway? Natalie hadn't even made the effort to attend her daughter's wedding. But then she hadn't made the effort to attend Merry's graduation or, indeed, any of the significant events that had marked her daughter's life.

Obsessed with the recollection of Roula's sleazy allegations, Merry was simply not in the mood to deal with her mother. Landing in London to discover that Angel had arranged to meet her for lunch had been unsettling. Merry was determined to confront him but only in her own time and only when she had decided exactly what she intended to say to him. Not yet at that point, she had ducked lunch and ignored his calls and texts. Let him fester for a while as she had had to fester while she'd run over Roula's claims until her head had ached and her stomach had been queasy and she had wept herself empty of tears.

Angel hadn't asked her to love him, she reminded herself as the limo drew up outside Sybil's house. But he had asked her to trust him and she had. Now that trust was broken and she was so wounded she felt as though she had been torn apart. She had trailed all her belongings and her daughter's back from Greece but she still didn't know what she would be doing next or even where she would be living. While she had been getting married, life had moved on. The cottage now had another tenant and she didn't want to move in with her aunt again. Nor did she want to feel like a sad, silly failure with Angel again.

'So glad you made the time to come,' Sybil gabbled almost nervously as Merry walked through the front door into the open-plan lounge where her mother rose stiffly upright to face her. Natalie bore little resemblance to her daughter, being small, blonde and rather plump, but she looked remarkably young for her forty odd years.

'Natalie,' Merry acknowledged, forcing herself forward to press an awkward kiss to her mother's cheek. 'How are you?'

'Oh, don't be all polite and nice as if we're strangers. That just makes me feel worse,' her mother immediately complained. 'Sybil has something to tell you. You had better sit down. It's going to come as a shock.'

Her brow furrowing in receipt of that warning, Merry sank down into an armchair and focused on her aunt. Sybil remained standing and she was very pale.

'We have a big secret in this family, which we have always covered up,' Sybil stated agitatedly. 'I didn't see much point in telling you about it so long after the event.'

'No, you never did like to tell anything that could make you look bad,' Natalie sniped. 'But you *promised* me that you would tell her.'

Sybil compressed her lips. 'When I was fifteen I got pregnant by a boy I was at school with. My parents were horrified. They sent me to live with a cousin up north and then they adopted my baby. It was all hushed up. I had to promise my mother that I would never tell my daughter the truth.'

Merry was bemused. 'I—'

'I was that adopted baby,' Natalie interposed thinly. 'I'm not Sybil's younger sister, I'm her *daughter* but I didn't find that out until I was eighteen.'

Losing colour, Merry flinched and focused on Sybil in disbelief. 'Your *daughter*?'

'Yes. Then my mother died and I felt that Natalie had the right to know who I really was. She was already talking about trying to trace her birth mother, so it seemed sensible to speak up before she tried doing that,' Sybil explained hesitantly.

'And overnight, when that truth came out, Sybil went from being my very exciting famous big sister, who gave me wonderful gifts, to being a liar, who had deceived me all my life,' Merry's mother condemned with a bitterness that shook Merry.

'So, you're actually my grandmother, not my

aunt,' Merry registered shakily as she studied Sybil and struggled to disentangle the family relationships she had innocently taken for granted.

'It wasn't my secret to share after the adoption. I gave up my rights but when I came clean about who I really was, it sent your mother off the rails.'

'Lies…the gift that keeps on giving,' Natalie breathed tersely. 'That's part of the reason I fell pregnant with you, Merry. When I had that stupid affair with your father, I was all over the place emotionally. I had lost my adoptive mother and then discovered that the sister I loved and admired was in fact my mother…and I didn't like her very much.'

'Natalie couldn't forgive me for putting my career first but it enabled me to give my parents enough money to live a very comfortable life while they raised my daughter,' Sybil argued in her own defence. 'I was grateful for their care of her. I wasn't ready to be a mother.'

'At least, not until *you* were born, Merry,' Natalie slotted in with perceptible scorn. 'Then Sybil interfered and stole you away from me.'

'It wasn't like that!' Sybil protested. 'You *needed* help.'

Merry's mother settled strained eyes on Merry's troubled face and said starkly, 'What do you think it was like for me to see *my* birth mother lavish-

ing all the love and care she had denied me on my
daughter instead?'

Merry breathed in deep and slow, struggling to
put her thoughts in order. In reality she was still
too upset about Roula's allegations to fully concentrate her brain on what the two women were telling her. Sybil was her grandmother, *not* her aunt
and Merry had never been told that Natalie was
an adopted child. She abhorred the fact that she
had not been given the full truth about her background sooner.

'The way Sybil treated you, the fuss she made
of you, made me *resent* you,' Merry's mother confessed guiltily. 'It wrecked our relationship. She
came between us.'

'That was never my intention,' Sybil declared
loftily.

'But that's how it was…' Natalie complained
stonily.

Merry lowered her head, recognising that she
saw points on both sides of the argument. Sybil
had only been fifteen when she gave Natalie up to
her parents for adoption and she had been barred
from admitting that she was Natalie's birth mum.
Merry refused to condemn Sybil for that choice
but she also saw how devastating that pretence
and the lies must've been for her own mother and

how finding out that truth years afterwards had distressed her.

'You *say* you want a closer relationship with me and yet you still had no interest in coming to my wedding or in meeting my daughter,' Merry heard herself fire back at her mother.

'I couldn't afford the plane fare!' Natalie snapped defensively. 'Who do you think paid for this visit?'

'How do you feel about this?' Sybil pressed anxiously.

'Confused,' Merry admitted tightly. 'Hurt that the two of you didn't tell me the truth years ago. And I hate lies, Sybil, and now I discover that you've pretty much been lying to me my whole life.'

In actuality, Merry felt as if the solid floor under her feet had fallen away, leaving her to stage a difficult balancing act. Her grandmother and her mother were both regarding her expectantly and she didn't know what she was supposed to say to satisfy either of them. The sad reality was that she had always had more in common with Sybil than with Natalie and that, no matter how hard she tried, she would probably never be able to replicate that close relationship with her mother.

'All I ever wanted to do was try to help you still have a life as a single parent,' Sybil told her daughter unhappily. 'You were so young. I never wanted to come between you and Merry.'

'I'd like to meet Elyssa,' Natalie declared. 'Sybil's shown me photos. She is very cute.'

And Merry realised then that she had been guilty of holding her own unstable childhood against her mother right into adulthood instead of accepting that Natalie might have changed and matured. 'I will bring her over for a visit,' she promised stiffly. 'How long are you staying for?'

'Two weeks,' Natalie told her. 'But now that Keith's gone and we've split up, I'm thinking of moving back to the UK again. I'd like to meet your husband while I'm here as well.'

Tears suddenly stinging her hot eyes, Merry nodded jerkily, not trusting herself to speak. She understood why her mother had wanted the story told but wasn't at all sure that she could give the older woman the warmer relationship she was clearly hoping for. But then too many of her emotions were bound up in the bombshell that had blown her marriage apart, she conceded guiltily. Roula's confession had devastated her and at that moment having to turn her back on the man she loved and her marriage was still all she could really think about. It was the thought, the terrifying awareness, of what she might have to do next that left room for nothing else and paralysed her.

She shared photos of the wedding and Elyssa with both women, glossed over Sybil's comment that she seemed very pale and quiet and returned to Foxcote Hall as soon as she decently could, having promised to bring Elyssa back for a visit within a few days. The limo travelled at a stately pace back up to the elegant country house that had the stunning architecture of an oversized Georgian dolls' house. Informal gardens shaded by clusters of mature trees spread out from the house and slowly changed into a landscape of green fields and lush stretches of woodland. Foxcote was a magnificent estate and yet Angel had not even mentioned that he owned a property near her aunt's home.

She had originally planned to go to a hotel from the airport, but when she had yet even to see and speak to Angel such a statement of separation had seemed a tad premature. Walking into the airy hall with its tall windows and tiled floor, she heard Elyssa chuckling and stringing together strings of nonsense words and she followed the sounds.

Several steps into the drawing room, she stopped dead because Angel was down on the floor with Elyssa, letting his daughter clamber over him and finally wrap her chubby arms round his neck and plant a triumphant noisy kiss on his face. He grinned, delighting in the baby's easy trusting affection, but his smile fell away the instant he glimpsed Merry. Suddenly his lean, darkly handsome features were sober and unsmiling, his beautiful dark eyes wary and intent.

'You never mentioned that you owned a house near Sybil's,' Merry remarked in a brittle voice as he vaulted lithely upright with Elyssa clasped to his chest.

'My father bought the estate when he was going through a hunting, shooting, fishing phase but he soon got bored. Angelina used it for a while when she was socialising with the heir to a local dukedom. It should really be sold now,' Angel contended, crossing the room to lift the phone and summon their nanny to take charge of their daughter.

A current of pained resentment bit into Merry when Elyssa complained bitterly about being separated from her father. That connection, that bond had formed much sooner than she had expected. Elyssa had taken to Angel like a duck to water, revelling in his more physical play and more boisterous personality. If her father was to disappear from her daily life, their daughter would miss him and be hurt by his absence. But then whose fault would that be? Merry asked herself angrily. It certainly wouldn't be *her* fault, she told herself piously. She had played by the rules. If their marriage broke down, it would be entirely Angel's responsibility.

'So, what's going on?' Angel enquired, taking up a faintly combative stance as Sally closed the door in her wake, his long powerful legs braced, shoulders thrown back, aggressive jaw line at an angle. 'You blew me off at lunch and all day you've been ignoring my calls and texts...*why*?'

Merry sucked in a steadying breath. 'I'm leaving you...well, in the process of it,' she qualified stiffly, her face pale and set.

'Why would you suddenly decide to leave me?' Angel demanded, striding forward, all brooding intimidation, dark eyes glittering like fireworks in the night sky. 'That makes no sense.'

Anger laced the atmosphere, tensing every defensive muscle in her body, and she cursed the reality that she was not mentally prepared for the confrontation about to take place.

'Roula told me everything.'

Angel looked bemused. 'Everything about... *what*?' he demanded with curt emphasis.

'That she's been your mistress for years, that you always go back to her eventually.'

'I don't have a mistress. I've never had one. Before you, I've never wanted repeat encounters with the same woman,' Angel told her almost conversationally, dark golden eyes locked to her strained face. 'You must've misunderstood something Roula said. There's no way that she told you that we were lovers.'

'There was no misunderstanding,' Merry framed stiffly. 'She was very frank about your relationship and about the fact that she expected it to continue even though you were married.'

'But it's not true. I don't know what she's playing at but her claims are nonsense,' Angel declared with harsh emphasis. 'Is this all we've got, Merry? Some woman only has to say I sleep with her and you swallow the story whole?'

Merry clasped her trembling hands together and tilted her chin, her spine rigid. 'She was very convincing. I believed her.'

'*Diavolos!* You just judge me out of hand? You believe her rather than *me*?' Angel raked at her in a burst of incredulous anger, black curls tumbling across his brow as he shook his head in evident disbelief. 'You take her word over mine?'

'She's your friend. Why would she lie about such a thing?'

'How the hell am I supposed to know?' Angel shot back at her. 'But she *is* lying!'

'She said you'd been lovers for years but that you've always had other women,' Merry recounted flatly. 'I will not accept you being with other women!'

Angel settled volatile eyes on her and she backed away a step at the sheer heat she met there.

'Then try not to *drive* me into being with them!' he slammed back. 'I have not been unfaithful to you.'

'She did say that you hadn't been with her since you got married but that eventually you would return to her because apparently you always do.'

'You are the only woman I have *ever* returned to!' Angel proclaimed rawly. 'I can't believe we're even having this stupid conversation—'

'It's not a conversation, it's an argument,' she interrupted.

'I promised you that there would be no other women,' Angel reminded her darkly. 'Didn't you listen? Obviously, you didn't believe—'

'Your reputation goes before you,' Merry flung back at him bitterly.

'I will not apologise for my past. I openly acknowledge it but I have never cheated on any woman I have been with!' Angel intoned in a driven undertone. 'I grew up with a mother who cheated on all her lovers and I lived with the consequences of that kind of behaviour. I know better. I'm honest and I move on when I get bored.'

'Well, maybe I don't want to hang around waiting for you to get bored with me and move on!' Merry fired back with ringing scorn. 'Maybe I think I'm worth more than that and deserve more respect. That's why I'm calling time on us now before things get messy!'

'You're not calling time on us. That's not your decision to make,' Angel delivered with lethal derision. 'We got married to make a home for our daughter and if we have to work at achieving that happy outcome, then we *work* at it.'

A cold, forlorn hollow spread like poison inside Merry's tight chest as she recognised how foolish and naïve she had been to dream that Angel could eventually come to care for her. He had only married her for Elyssa's sake. She would never be important to him in her own right, never be that one special woman in his eyes, never be anything other than second best to him. He could have had any woman, and a woman like Roula Paulides, who shared his background and nationality as well as a long friendship with him, would have had infinitely more to offer him. He wouldn't have had to talk about having to *work* at being married to anyone else. In fact her mind boggled at the concept of Angel being prepared to do anything as dully conventional and sensible as *work* at a relationship.

'I don't want to work at it,' she heard herself say, and it was truthfully what she felt at that moment because her pride could not bear the idea of him having to suppress his natural instincts before he could accept being married to her and staying faithful.

'You don't get a choice,' Angel spelled out grimly. 'We'll fly back to Palos in the morning—'

'No!' she interrupted. 'I'm not returning to Greece with you!'

'You're my wife and you're not leaving me,' Angel asserted harshly. 'That isn't negotiable.'

Merry tossed her head, dark hair rippling back from her flushed cheeks, pale blue eyes icy with fury. 'I'm not even trying to negotiate with you... I already know what a slippery slope that can be. Our marriage is over and I'm staying in the UK,' she declared fiercely. 'I'll move out of here as soon as I decide where I'm going to be living.'

Angel stared back at her, his hard bone structure prominent below his bronzed skin, his eyes very dark and hard. 'You would just throw everything we've got away?' he breathed in a tone of suppressed savagery that made her flinch. 'And what about our daughter?'

Merry swallowed with difficulty, sickly envisioning the likely battle ahead and cringing from the prospect. 'I'll fight you for custody of our daughter here in the UK,' she told him squarely, shocked at what she was saying but needing to convince him that she would not be softened or sidelined by threats.

Angel froze almost as if she had struck him, black lashes lifting on grim dark eyes without the smallest shade of gold, his lean, strong face rigid with tension. 'You would separate us? That I will not forgive you for,' he told her with fierce finality.

Ten seconds later, Merry was alone in the room, listening numbly to the roar of a helicopter taking off somewhere nearby and presumably ferrying Angel back to London. And she was in shock, her head threatening to explode with the sheer unbearable pressure that had built up inside it, her stomach churning sickly. Tears surged in a hot stinging tide into her eyes and she blinked furiously but the tears kept on coming, dripping down her face.

Their marriage was over. Hadn't she always feared that their marriage wouldn't last? Why was she so shocked? Yes, he had denied that Roula Paulides was his mistress but she hadn't believed him, had she? When she had packed her bags on the island she had known she wasn't coming back and certainly not to a marriage with a husband who had to *work* at being married to her!

CHAPTER TEN

MISERY AND GUILT kept Merry awake for half the night. She had threatened Angel just as he had once threatened her and now it lay like a big rock of shame on her conscience because she had witnessed the depth of his attachment to Elyssa, had watched it develop, had even noticed how surprised Angel was at the amount of enjoyment he received from being a parent. He did not love his wife but he definitely *did* love his daughter.

All her emotions in free fall after the sensitive family issues that had been explored at Sybil's house, she had been in no fit state to deal with Angel. She had drawn up battle lines for a war she didn't actually want to wage, she acknowledged wretchedly. A divorce or separation didn't have to be bitter and nasty and she hadn't the smallest desire for them to fight like cat and dog over their daughter. Angel was a good father, a *very* good father and she would never try to deprive him of con-

tact with his child. Just because she couldn't trust
him with the Roulas of the world didn't mean she
was blind to his skills as a parent or that she wasn't
aware that Elyssa benefitted as much as Angel did
from their relationship. She wasn't that selfish, that
prejudiced against him, *was* she?

Anguish screamed through her as she sniffed
and blew her nose over her breakfast in the dining room. She was a garish match for her elegantly
furnished surroundings, clad as she was in comfy
old pyjamas and a silky, boldly patterned kimono
robe that had seen better days. She had left her
fancy new wardrobe behind on Palos as a statement of rejection that she wanted Angel to notice.
She had wanted him to appreciate that she didn't
need him or his money or those stupid designer
clothes, even if that was a lie.

Her real problem, however, was that pain and
hurt magnified everything and distorted logic. She
had told Angel that she was leaving him because
pride had demanded she act as though she were
strong and decisive rather than betray the reality
that she was broken up and confused and horri-
bly hurt.

The thwack-thwack of a helicopter coming into
land made her head ache even more and she gulped
down more tea, desperate to soothe her ragged
nerves. She heard the slam of the front door and

she stiffened, her head jerking up as the dining-room door opened without warning and framed Angel's tall, powerful form. She could not have been more appalled had he surprised her naked because she knew she looked like hell. Her eyes and nose were red, her hair was tangled.

'Will you come into the drawing room?' Angel asked grimly. 'There's someone here to see you.'

'I'm not dressed,' she protested stiltedly, her head lowering to hide her face as she stumbled upright, desperate to make a quick escape from his astute gaze.

'You'll do fine,' Angel told her callously, dark eyes cold and treacherous as black ice.

'I can't see anyone looking like this,' Merry argued vehemently, striving to leave the room and flee upstairs by sidestepping him, but she found him as immoveable in the doorway as a rock.

'You'll be in very good company. I swear she's cried all the way from Greece,' Angel informed her incomprehensibly, gripping her elbow with a firm hand and practically thrusting her into the room next door.

Merry's feet froze to the floor when she saw the woman standing by the window. It was Roula, looking something less than her usually sophisti-cated and stylish self. Her ashen complexion only emphasised her swollen eyes and pink nose and she was convulsively shredding a tissue between her restive fingers.

'I'm so...*so* sorry!' she gasped, facing Merry. 'I lied to you.'

Angel shot something at the other woman in irate Greek and she groaned and snapped something back, and then the door closed behind Merry and when she turned her head again, Angel was gone, leaving them alone.

'You *lied* to me?' Merry prompted in astonishment.

'I was trying to frighten you off. I thought if you left him he might finally turn to me,' Roula framed shakily, her voice hoarse with embarrassment and misery.

'Oh,' Merry mumbled rather blankly. 'You're not his mistress, then?'

'No, that was nonsense,' Roula framed hoarsely. 'We've never had sex either. Angel's never been interested in me that way, but because we were such good friends I thought if you broke up with him he would confide in me and maybe start seeing me in a different light. But it's not going to happen. He said the idea of me and him ever being intimate was disgusting, *incestuous*. I wish I'd worked out that that's how he saw me years ago. I'd have saved myself a lot of heartache.'

Merry experienced a very strong desire to pat

the blonde's shoulder to comfort her and had to fight the weird prompting off. She could see that the other woman felt humiliated and guilty and very sad. 'Did Angel force you to come here and tell me this?'

'Well, it wasn't my idea, but he said I owed him and he was right. From the moment he told me that he was marrying you I was so *jealous* of you!' Roula confessed with a sudden wrenching sob, clamping her hand to her mouth and getting herself back under control again before continuing, 'Why you? I asked myself. Why *not* me? You worked for him and he never ever sleeps with his employees and yet he slept with *you*...and you've got a great figure and you're very pretty but you're not exactly supermodel material...and then you totally freak him out by having a baby and yet somehow he's now crazy about the baby as well!'

'Have you always been in love with him?' Merry mumbled uncomfortably, grasping that, by Roula's reckoning, Angel deciding to marry her qualified as an unbelievable and quite undeserved miracle.

'When I was a teenager it was just a crush. He was my best friend. I knew all the rotten things Angelina has ever done to him and it broke my heart. I learned how to handle her to keep her out of his hair, to try and help him cope with her.

That's why she likes me, that's why she decided that he should marry me if he ever married anyone. I've had other relationships, of course,' Roula told her wryly. 'But every time one broke down, I told myself it would've been different with Angel. He was my ideal, my Mr Right…at least he was until he dragged me onto that plane and shouted at me half the night!'

'His temper's rough,' Merry conceded while frantically trying to work out how she had so badly misjudged the man whom she had married. It was obvious that Roula was now telling her the truth. Bitter jealousy had driven the blonde into an attempt to destroy Angel's marriage.

'And he's like the elephant who never forgets when you cross him. He'll never forgive me for causing all this trouble,' Roula muttered with weary regret.

'He'll get over it,' Molly said woodenly, wondering if he would ever forgive her either.

'I'm sorry. I'm truly sorry,' the blonde framed guiltily. 'I know that's not much consolation in the circumstances but I deeply regret lying to you. I didn't think it through. I told myself you'd probably got deliberately pregnant and planned the whole thing to trap him. I could see he was happy on your wedding day but I wouldn't admit that to myself and if anyone merits being happy, it's Angel.'

'I think we can forget about this now,' Merry commented uncomfortably. 'I can't put my hand on my heart and say that I forgive you, but I am grateful you explained why you did it and I do understand.'

'Fair enough,' Roula sighed as she opened the door to leave.

Merry tensed when she saw Angel poised across the hall, straightening to his full predatory height, shrewd dark eyes scanning her like a radiation counter.

'I told the truth,' Roula told him flatly. 'Can I leave now?'

'You're satisfied?' Angel demanded of Merry.

She nodded in embarrassed confirmation.

'I'll have you returned to the airport,' Angel informed Roula curtly.

Merry took advantage of his momentary inattention to head for the stairs at a very fast rate of knots. She wanted to splash her face, clean her teeth, brush her hair and ditch the pyjamas with the pink bunny rabbits on them. Then she would work out what she had to say to him to redress the damage she had done with her lack of faith. Possibly a spot of grovelling would be appropriate, obviously a heartfelt apology...

She was caught unprepared and halfway into a pair of jeans when Angel strode into the bedroom. He thrust the door shut, leant his long, lean frame sinuously back against it and studied her with brooding dark eyes.

'I'm sorry... I'm really sorry,' she muttered, yanking up the jeans. 'But she was very convincing and I don't think she's a bad person. I think she was just jealous and she got a bit carried away.'

'I don't give a damn about Roula or why she did what she did,' Angel declared impatiently. 'I care that even after being married to me for weeks you were still willing to threaten me with the loss of my daughter.'

Merry lost colour, her eyes guiltily lowering from the hard challenge of his. 'That was wrong,' she acknowledged ruefully. 'But you used the same threat to persuade me into marrying you...or have you forgotten that?'

'My intentions were good. I wanted to persuade you to give us a chance to be a proper family. But your intentions were bad and destructive,' Angel countered without hesitation. 'You wanted to use Elyssa like a weapon to punish me. That would have damaged her as much as me.'

'No, I honestly wasn't thinking like that,' Merry argued, turning her back to him to flip off the despised pyjama top and reaching for a tee shirt, having decided for the sake of speed and dignity to forgo donning a bra. 'Even when I was mad at you

I accepted that you are a great father, but I assumed you would make any divorce a bitter, nasty battle.'

'What made you assume that?' Angel asked drily. 'I didn't even ask you to sign a pre-nuptial agreement before the wedding. That omission sent the family lawyers into a tailspin but it was a deliberate move on my part. It was an act of faith formed on my foolish assumption that you would respect our marriage as much as I did.'

Merry reddened with more guilt. He really knew what buttons to push, she reflected wretchedly. It hadn't occurred to her that he hadn't asked her to sign a pre-nup before the ceremony, but in retrospect she could see that that had been a glaring omission, indeed a very positive statement, in a marriage involving a very wealthy man and a reasonably poor woman. His continuing coldness was beginning to unnerve her. He had never used that tone with her before. He sounded detached and negative and he was still icily angry. She glanced up, scanning his lean, strong features for another, more encouraging reading of his mood, and instead noted the forbidding line of his wide, sensual mouth, the harsh angle of his firm jaw and the level darkness of his accusing gaze.

'But the instant we hit the first rough patch in our marriage you were ready to throw it all away,' Angel condemned.

'A long-term mistress is more than a rough patch,' Merry protested helplessly. 'I believed Roula because you introduced me to her as a friend that you trusted.'

'She's the sister I never had,' Angel asserted with sardonic bite. 'The thought of anything of a sexual nature between us is…repellent.'

And the last piece of the puzzle fell into place for Merry, who, while believing Roula, had not quite been able to grasp why Angel had never been tempted into having a more intimate relationship with her. After all, Roula was a beauty and had to share a lot with him. But if he saw the blonde in the same light as a sibling, his indifference to her as a woman was instantly understandable and highly unlikely to ever change.

'I've seen a lot of divorces,' Angel admitted. 'In my own family, amongst friends. Nobody comes out unscathed but the children suffer the most. I don't want my daughter to ever suffer that damage, but neither do I want a wife who runs like a rabbit at the first sign of trouble.'

'I did *not* run like a rabbit!' Merry argued, hot-faced. 'Maybe you're thinking of what you did after I told you I was pregnant!'

'I took responsibility. I ensured your financial needs were covered.'

'But you weren't there when I was throwing

up every morning and trying to drag myself into work to keep my job.'

'You didn't need to keep on working. Your allowance would have covered your living costs.' Angel hesitated before asking with a frown, 'Were you sick that often?'

'Every day for about four months, often more than once a day. And then one evening I started bleeding and I assumed I was having a miscarriage. After that, I resigned from my job and went home to stay with Sybil.'

Angel levered his long, lean frame lithely off the door, moving with that innate grace of his towards her, his lean, dark face troubled. 'You almost lost Elyssa?'

'Well, I *thought* I was losing her and I panicked and went to the hospital, but it was just one of those pregnancy mishaps that seem more serious than they are. It was very frightening, though, and very upsetting.'

'And I wasn't there when I should've been,' Angel registered for himself, studying her grimly. 'Can't turn the clock back and be there for you either, so that can't be changed. Do you think you will always hold my absence during those months against me?'

'I try not to dwell on it. If you didn't want a relationship with me at the time there would've been no point in you coming back into my life,' she conceded simply. 'It would've been too awkward for both of us.'

Angel winced. 'I didn't even realise that I *did* want to be in a relationship with you back then. I would have to admit that I was completely blind to my own hang-ups. Growing up I only saw shallow, chaotic relationships, which is why when I was an adult I avoided anything that could have been construed as a relationship. I had sex and that was that, end of...only then I met you and my blueprint for a relaxed and unemotional life went up in flames.'

'How could you have an unemotional life when you're so full of emotion?' Merry asked him incredulously.

'I keep that side of me under control...at least I did until you and Elyssa sneaked through my defences,' Angel reasoned wryly. 'You know, you may not have been a happy camper while you were pregnant but I wasn't any happier. You shook me up. You made me want more and that scared me because I had no experience of a normal relationship.'

'You don't do relationships,' she reminded him drily.

'What have I been doing with you for the past month?' Angel shot back at her. 'There's nothing casual about our connection. Do you really think it's normal for me to be content to spend so much time with one woman?'

'I didn't ask you to do that.'

'I'm a selfish bastard. I did it only because I wanted to.'

'For your daughter's sake, you *worked* at being married to me,' Merry paraphrased with pained dismissiveness.

Angel shook his arrogant dark head in wonderment. 'I've got to admit that right now I'm having to *work* at being married to you because you are so stubbornly determined to think the worst of me.'

'That's not true.'

'You don't trust me. You're always waiting for the roof to fall in! I used to think that was cute but now I'm beginning to wonder if you'll ever recognise that, even though I've made a hell of a lot of mistakes along the way, I do love you,' he completed almost defiantly.

Merry stared at him in astonishment. 'You don't.'

'Even when you're wearing the bunny pyjamas you were wearing the night I got you pregnant,' Angel assured her with confidence. 'I didn't recognise it as love until after we were married. Even though I'm always worrying about you, I'm incredibly happy being with you. I wake up in the morning and everything feels good because you're there beside me. When you're not there, everything feels *off* and I feel weirdly lonely…'

Merry's lower lip parted company with her upper and she stared at him in wide-eyed consternation.

'And the most extraordinary thing of all is that I thought you loved me too until you walked out and accused me of cheating on you,' Angel admitted ruefully. 'I thought that for the first time in my life I was loved for who I was, not for what I can do or buy or provide. You know I'm flawed and you accept it. You know I'm still finding my way in this family set-up.'

'You're not the only one. Yesterday I discovered that Sybil is not my aunt but my grandmother,' Merry told him in a sudden surge. 'That's another reason why I was so upset and over the top with you yesterday. I was already all shaken up. My mother was adopted by Sybil's parents and only learned the truth when she was eighteen. Oh, never mind, I'll explain it all to you later, but finding out that Sybil and Natalie had been keeping all that from me all my life made me feel deceived…and you're right, I *do* love you,' she completed almost apologetically. 'I have almost from the start. Don't know why, don't know how, just got attached regardless of common sense.'

Angel rested his hands down on her taut shoulders. 'We had an electric connection from the first day. Somehow, we match. I just wish I hadn't wasted so much time staying away from you when I wanted to be with you. I was existing in a sort of fog of denial that everything had changed and that I wanted the sort of relationship that I had never trusted or experienced with a woman.'

'And I let you down,' she whispered guiltily. 'I did think the worst at the first sign of trouble. I wasn't strong and sensible the way I should have been.'

'It's sort of comforting that your common sense leaves you when you're upset. When I arrived and saw you'd been crying, obviously upset, it gave me hope that you did care.'

'I'll always care,' she muttered softly, turning her cheek into the caress of his long fingers.

'I've never trusted love. I know my father cares about me but my mother lost interest the minute I grew beyond the cute baby stage,' he confided. 'What you said about Sybil and your mother? Take it back to basics, *agape mou*. You may not have known the whole story but you were *always* loved. That's a blessing. It's much harder to love without that experience and the confidence it gives you.'

Merry stretched up to him and buried her face in his shoulder, drinking in the musky familiar aroma of his skin like a restorative drug. He caught her chin in his fingers and tipped up her mouth to taste her with hungry urgency.

'You taste so good,' he ground out, walking her back towards the bed with single-minded intent. 'Tell me you love me again… I like hearing it.'

'How did you guess how I felt?' Merry pressed. 'I thought I was hiding it.'

'You put up with all my unreasonable demands and still smiled at me. I didn't deserve it so there had to be some other reason why you were being so tolerant and sometimes I couldn't help testing you to see if you'd crack.'

'I don't crack. I'm loyal and loving…as long as you don't take on a mistress.'

'Where would I get the energy?' Angel growled, his attention elsewhere as he slid his hand below the tee shirt to mould it to a plump breast with satisfaction, and then wrenched her out of its concealment with unashamed impatience. '*Thee mou*, I want you so much it hurts… I thought I was losing you.'

'And then I disappointed you.'

'You're not supposed to walk away, you're supposed to stand and fight for me,' Angel told her. 'I fought for you.'

'I was hiding behind my pride.'

'I don't have any where you're concerned and I have even fewer scruples. I was willing to drug and kidnap you to get you back to Greece. You don't want to know the things that ran through my mind when I thought I was losing you,' he assured her. 'A large helping of crazy, if I'm honest.'

'That's because you love me,' Merry told him happily. 'You're allowed to think crazy things if you want to fight to keep me...'

And their clothes fell away in a messy heap as Angel moved to make her his again and satisfy the last lurking stab of insecurity inside him. Merry was his again and all was right with his world, well, almost all. He shifted lithely against her, holding her close.

'When you feel up to the challenge, we'll have another baby and I will share the whole experience with you,' Angel promised, jolting her out of her drowsy sensual daydream.

'*Another*...baby?' Merry gasped in disbelief. 'You've got to be kidding! Elyssa's only seven months old!'

'You could consider it...eventually, hopefully,' Angel qualified. 'Although I'll settle for Elyssa if you don't want another child. It's not a deal breaker.'

'Are you sure the threat of that extra responsibility won't make you run for the hills again?' Merry asked snidely.

'No, set me the challenge of getting you pregnant and I assure you that I will happily meet every demand, no matter how strenuous or time consuming it becomes.' Dark golden eyes alive with tender amusement, Angel gazed down with a wide, relaxed smile. 'In fact I find the concept quite exciting.'

Merry punched a bare brown shoulder in reproach. 'Anything to do with sex excites you!'

Angel looked reflective and a sudden wicked grin lit his darkly handsome features. 'I'm sure if we had about six children, six very *noisy* and *lively* children, I could persuade my mother to find her own accommodation. You see, expansion could be a complete game changer in the happy-family stakes...'

'I do hope that was a joke,' Merry sighed, warm and contented and so happy she felt floaty. He loved her and it shone out of him. How had she not seen that? How had she tormented herself for so long when what she desperately wanted was right there in front of her, waiting to be claimed?

And now Angel was hers, finally all hers, and equally suddenly she was discovering that she was feeling much more tolerant and forgiving of other people's frailties. Her mother was trying to show her that she cared and perhaps it was past time she made more of an effort in that quarter. And then there was Roula, unhappy and humiliated—possibly she could afford to be more forgiving there as well. Happiness could spread happiness, she decided cheerfully, running a seeking hand down over a long, sleek male flank, keen to increase his happiness factor too...

'Well, I have to confess that I never saw this coming,' Natalie admitted, studying her mother, Sybil, and Angel's father, Charles, as they stood across the room graciously receiving the guests at the wedding reception being held at Angel and Merry's home on the island of Palos. 'I thought it would fizzle out long before they got this far.'

'He's daft about her and she has made him wait six years to put that ring on her finger,' Merry reminded the small blonde woman by her side. 'I think she's just finally ready to settle down.'

'Well, she took her time about it,' Natalie pronounced wryly. 'Angel's mother isn't here, is she?'

'Hardly, considering that she was Charles' first wife,' Merry remarked.

'Not much chance of *her* settling down.'

'No,' Merry agreed quietly, reflecting that they saw remarkably little of Angelina these days. Angelina had bought a Manhattan penthouse where she now spent most of her time. Occasional scandalous headlines and gossip pieces floated back to Angel and Merry, but Angel was no longer forced to be involved in his mother's life and now found it easier to remain detached.

Elyssa rushed up, an adorable vision in a pink flower girl's dress that already had a stain on it. 'Keep this for me,' she urged, stuffing the little wicker basket she had carried down the aisle into her mother's hand. 'Cos and I are going to play hide and seek.'

Merry bent down. 'No, you're not. This is a very special party for grown-ups and children aren't allowed to run about.'

Her son, Cosmas, four years old to his big sister's almost six years, rushed up, wrenching impatiently at the sash tied round his waist. 'Take this off.'

'Not until Sybil says you can,' Merry warned. 'There are still photos to be taken.'

'Where's the rest of the horde?' Natalie enquired curiously.

Their two-year-old twins, Nilo and Leksi, were chasing Tiger through the hall. Merry hurtled in that direction to interrupt the chase before it got out of hand. Tiger was a mere shadow of the fat and inactive little dog he had once been. Living in a household with five children had slimmed him down. His first rehoming hadn't worked out and when he had been returned to Sybil soon afterwards, after shaming himself and stealing food,

Merry had scooped him up for a rapturous reunion and brought him back to Greece. As she hovered Angel appeared, a baby clutched securely below one arm, and spoke sternly to his youngest sons. Atlanta beamed gummily across the hall at her mother and opened her arms.

'I don't know where you get the energy,' Natalie confessed, watching Merry reclaim her eight-month-old daughter. 'Either of you. You produce like rabbits. Please tell me the family's complete now.'

Colour warmed Merry's cheeks because their sixth child was already on the way, even if they had not yet announced the fact, and Angel grinned down at his tongue-tied wife with wicked amusement. 'We haven't decided yet,' he said lightly.

Atlanta tugged on her mother's long hair as Merry walked out onto the terrace to take a break from the festivities. It had taken weeks of careful planning to organise the wedding and accommodation for all the guests. She had wanted everything to be perfect for Sybil and Charles, both of whom were frequent visitors to their home. After all the years of feeling short-changed in the family stakes, Merry had come full circle and now she was surrounded by a loving family.

She was even happier to have achieved a more normal relationship with her mother, who had returned to the UK and started up a very successful yoga studio. These days she regularly saw Natalie when she went over to London with Angel. Her mother had mellowed and Merry had put the past behind her in every way.

A year earlier she had acted as Roula's matron of honour when the other woman had married the island doctor in a three-day-long bout of very Greek celebration. Roula was still a friend of the family, and sometimes Merry suspected that the trouble the other woman had caused with the mistress lie and the truths that had then come out had actually helped Roula to move on and meet someone capable of loving her back.

But then Merry was willing to admit that she had learned from the same experience as well. Discovering that she was married to a man who loved her so much that he was willing to do virtually anything it took to hang onto her and their marriage had banished her insecurity for ever. She liked being a mother and Angel revelled in being a father. The rapid expansion of their family had been exhausting but also uniquely satisfying.

Lean brown hands scooped the slumbering baby from Merry's lap and passed her to Jill, Sally's conanny, for attention. Angel then scooped his wife out of her chair and sank back down with her cradled in his arms.

'You are very tired,' he scolded. 'We've talked about this. You agreed to take afternoon naps.'

'After the meal,' she murmured, small fingers flirting with his silk tie as she gazed up at him, loving and appreciating every line of his lean, startlingly handsome features and thinking back lazily to the poor beginning they had shared that had miraculously transformed over the years into a glorious partnership.

'Thee mou,' Angel intoned huskily. 'Sometimes I look at the life you have created for all of us and I love you so much it hurts, *agape mou*. My wife, my family, is my anchor.'

Happy as a teenager in his public display of affection where once she would have wrenched herself free, Merry giggled. 'You mean we drag you down?'

And Angel gave up the battle and kissed her, hungrily, deeply, tenderly while somewhere in the background his mother-in-law snorted and said in a pained voice, 'You see…like rabbits.'

* * * * *

If you enjoyed
THE SECRET VALTINOS BABY
why not explore these other
Lynne Graham stories?

HIS QUEEN BY DESERT DECREE
CLAIMED FOR THE LEONELLI LEGACY
SOLD FOR THE GREEK'S HEIR

Available now!

And look out for the rest of Lynne's
VOWS FOR BILLIONAIRES trilogy
coming soon!

#3605 HIRED FOR ROMANO'S PLEASURE
by Chantelle Shaw

Orla *never* forgot Torre's cruel rejection, or the white-hot pleasure they found together! Working late nights with him is sensual torture—and Torre is tempting Orla to play with fire once again...

#3606 CONTRACTED FOR THE PETRAKIS HEIR
One Night With Consequences
by Annie West

As Alice defiantly informs Adoni Petrakis of her pregnancy, memories of his skilled touch overwhelm her! His contract to claim her is shocking—so is realizing she's inescapably in his thrall!

#3607 CLAIMED BY HER BILLIONAIRE PROTECTOR
by Robyn Donald

Elana Grange isn't prepared for Niko Radcliffe's heart-stopping charisma. Their chemistry is electrifying, especially when circumstances force them together. Niko's embrace promises ecstasy, but letting him close feels so very dangerous...

#3608 CONVENIENT BRIDE FOR THE KING
Claimed by a King
by Kelly Hunter

King Theodosius needs a queen to keep his throne. So Theo makes Princess Moriana an offer she can't refuse—an initiation in the pleasures of the marriage bed...

Get 2 Free Books,
Plus 2 Free Gifts —

just for trying the
Reader Service!

HP17R3

Rocco was going to kiss her, and after everything she'd just said, Nicole knew she needed to stop him. But suddenly she found herself governed by a much deeper need than preserving her sanity or her pride. A need and a hunger that swept over her with the speed of a bushfire. As Rocco's shadowed face lowered toward her, she found past and present fusing, so that for a disconcerting moment she forgot everything except the urgent hunger in her body. Because hadn't her Sicilian husband always been able to do this—to captivate her with the lightest touch and to tantalize her with that smoldering look of promise? And hadn't there been many nights since they'd separated when she'd woken up, still half muddled with sleep, and found herself yearning for the taste of his lips on hers just one more time? And now she had it.

One more time.

She opened her mouth—though afterward she would try to

convince herself she'd been intending to resist him—but Rocco used the opportunity to fasten his mouth over hers in the most perfect of fits. And Nicole felt instantly helpless—caught up in the powerful snare of a sexual mastery that wiped out everything else. She gave a gasp of pleasure because it had been so long since she had done this.

Since they'd been apart Nicole had felt like a living statue—as if she were made from marble, as if the flesh-and-blood parts of her were some kind of half-forgotten dream. Slowly but surely she had withdrawn from the sensual side of her nature, until she'd convinced herself she was dead and unfeeling inside. But here came Rocco to wake her dormant sexuality with nothing more than a single kiss. It was like some stupid fairy story. It was scary and powerful. She didn't want to want him, and yet…

She wanted him.

Her lips opened wider as his tongue slid inside her mouth, eagerly granting him that intimacy as if preparing the way for another. She began to shiver as his hands started to explore her—rediscovering her body with an impatient hunger, as if it were the first time he'd ever touched her.

"Nicole," he said unevenly. She'd never heard him say her name like that before.

Her arms were locked behind his neck as again he circled his hips in unmistakable invitation and, somewhere in the back of her mind, Nicole could hear the small voice of reason imploring her to take control of the situation. It was urging her to pull back from him and call a halt to what they were doing. But once again she ignored it. Against the powerful tide of passion, that little voice was drowned out and she allowed pleasure to shimmer over her skin.

Don't miss
BOUND TO THE SICILIAN'S BED
available March 2018 wherever
Harlequin Presents® books and ebooks are sold.

www.Harlequin.com

Coming next month: a scandalous story of passion and pregnancy!

In *Contracted for the Petrakis Heir* by Annie West, Alice Trehearn has just discovered she's pregnant— and Adoni is determined to legally bind her to him!

A positive pregnancy test isn't the only reminder Alice has of her one scorching night with Adoni Petrakis. As she defiantly tells him the news, memories of his skilled touch overwhelm her! The contract he draws up to claim her and his child is utterly shocking. As is her realization that she's still powerfully, inescapably, in thrall to this vengeful Greek!

Contracted for the Petrakis Heir
One Night With Consequences

Available March 2018

HPBPA0218

Want to give in to temptation with
steamy tales of irresistible desire?

Check out **Harlequin® Presents®**,
Harlequin® Desire and
Harlequin® Kimani™ Romance books!

New books available every month!

CONNECT WITH US AT:

Harlequin.com/Community

Facebook.com/HarlequinBooks

Twitter.com/HarlequinBooks

Instagram.com/HarlequinBooks

Pinterest.com/HarlequinBooks

ReaderService.com

**ROMANCE WHEN
YOU NEED IT**

PGENRE2017